# Three Simple Rules

Brian Perry

**Three Simple Rules**

First Edition: 2022

ISBN: 9781524318178
ISBN eBook: 9781524328290

# Table of Contents

# Chapter 1

It was hard to get motivated that morning. Ashley just wanted to stay in bed. The radio said the temperature outside was negative fifteen with a windchill of thirty-five below. She knew she had to get up and get going, but had absolutely no motivation to step out into the frigid morning. She was too comfortable and warm wrapped in her special blanket. Her mother had given her that blanket on her wedding day, and she had kept and cherished it ever since.

Her father had died in an industrial accident when she was only three, and she had no memory of him. Her mother, Sonja, had raised her until she was thirteen. That is when she met Garry. They dated for a while and got married when Ashley was sixteen. He was a great stepfather. Over time, she even felt he was a great father. He took her fishing at the park and taught her to dance and how to stand up for herself. He hunted, fished, enjoyed sports, and helped teach her those. The only two things that she excelled in and enjoyed was the fishing and watching baseball. She could gut a deer and process the meat, but felt they were too pretty to eat. He got her into softball, in which her team got state championship. He would interview and interrogate the boys she would bring home throughout high school.

Her freshman year of college, she met Sarah in one of her classes, and they quickly became friends. After a month or so, Sarah introduced her to her brother, Mark. They hit it off great, just like old friends. They had coffee at the Quad, sodas at dinner on campus, and had even fallen asleep together in the library, before Mark had been taken home for Garry's approval. Even though it was a mere formality, she trusted Garry's opinion, and she loved him as a father. She warned Mark about Garry before getting his approval to date.

As the alarm sounded for the third time, she finally turned it off, wishing she had hit snooze again. She knew the day had to start; people were depending on her. As she got up, she thought a nice hot bath would be the best way to start her day.

As she lay soaking in the tub, relaxing, her phone rang. She knew it was probably Tim calling, making sure she was awake on such a blistery morning. She had prepared for this inevitability and had placed her cell phone on the rim of her soaker tub.

"Good morning, Tim." She spoke in a hushed tone.

"Good morning, Beautiful. Are you up and at 'em?" he asked in a heavy southern accent.

"Just stepping out of the bath," she replied knowing how crazy that would make him.

She had been dating Tim for about three years now, but knew him before the accident took her husband's life three years ago. It had been another cold wintry day in January. Her husband Mark had gotten a call from his sister telling him she was in labor; he had rushed to get to the hospital in time to see his newborn nephew. He wanted to be the first in the family to see him. On his way there, he lost control of his car and crossed into oncoming traffic. He was killed instantly. They had only been married for six months.

"Have mercy on the fly on the wall," he said with a laugh, "I wish I was that fly. Seeing you in the tub. . ."

"Tim," she interrupted, "I will see you tonight, I have to get dried off and dressed so I can get to work on time. It is already six o'clock."

After she hung up the phone, she drained the tub and dried off. She dressed and went down stairs to make her breakfast. That morning, she made two scrambled eggs and toast. After a glance at her kitchen clock, she knew she had to hurry; it was already seven in the morning.

She arrived at work with only minutes to spare, thankful she had gotten a new battery in the car only the day before. This was going to be a good Monday, she thought to herself as she walked in the doors. Her day went pretty much as she thought it would: meetings, expense reports, and shuffling papers—enough to make her glad when five o'clock came around. She was looking forward to dinner with Tim as she clocked out and headed towards her car.

The words Tim had spoken to her that morning had helped her get through her boring day. She kept imagining the look on his face when she could finally wake up to him lying next to her in bed.

"I wish he had been a fly on the wall this morning," she spoke aloud as she started her car and exited the parking garage.

The two had made plans to meet for dinner and drinks that night at Rusty's Restaurant over the weekend, and she relished seeing him. Tonight was their three-year anniversary. She knew he would be waiting at their favorite table and she spotted him immediately as she entered. He was dressed in a black business suit and held a dozen red roses. He looked up and smiled as she entered the establishment.

"You look ravishing," he said as she arrived at the table. "And you're late."

"I had to go home and change. I couldn't see such a dashing hunk in my work attire," she responded as he pulled out her chair.

She had dressed her petite, 135-pound, five-foot-six frame, with a green velvety dress that stopped just short of her knees. Her long, strawberry-blonde hair was set free and fell to the middle of her back. She had a hard time pretending other men didn't notice her. Tim had never seen the dress before and would definitely remember it from now on. It was tight in all the right places and enhanced her bosom.

"Did you paint it on yourself or did someone help you?" he asked with a slight chuckle.

"You don't like it?" she replied. "I can take it off, you know."

"I would love to see that."

His spoken word was soft and sexy, making her blush. The sexual tension between them was obvious to everyone in the restaurant that night. After dinner, he walked her to her car and kissed her goodnight and asked her to call him when she made it home, using the weather as an excuse.

After an hour drive to her house, she pulled off the road. She saw a deer run through the woods, across her driveway. Her house sat about one thousand feet off the road, surrounded by dense trees. It was a large house, two story, and just shy of five thousand square feet of living space with a wraparound porch and a finished basement. She always felt guilty coming home. Guilty, because Mark's life insurance money had paid for his dream house she solely now occupied. Their dreams of hearing the pitter patter of little feet obliterated on that fateful day. She felt guilty about not having children herself and guilty because she lived on the one hundred acres of land. Mark had come from money and had a great job, so he could afford the $2 million life insurance policy that bought her all of this. She missed Mark, but was sure she was falling in love with Tim.

Upon entering the house, she called Sarah and told her about their date.

Sarah and Ashley remained best friends since the passing of Mark. Then, she did as she had been asked and called Tim. He answered on the first ring.

"I was starting to get worried about you," he stated.

"You know it takes me a while to get home from town," she said.

"Yeppers, about an hour from town, up in the hills. All alone. Maybe a strapping young man should come out and make sure the house is safe and no vermin got in there for you," he said, allowing his accent to thicken as he spoke.

He had been to her house before but not since they started dating. She felt it would be wrong for him to come over to what she still thought of as her and Mark's house. They always met up at their destination, and never at either one's home. In fact, she didn't even know where he was living and that is the way she wanted it to remain. All she knew was he had a two-bedroom apartment and if she wanted to stay the night, she could always use the second bedroom. He had offered many times, always to a polite refusal.

They chatted on the phone for about an hour. Then she finally told him goodnight. She curled up in her favorite blanket and drifted off to sleep.

The next few months went pretty much the same. They usually saw each other on Friday and Saturday nights. He would call in the mornings. Then came a spring day when she awoke before her alarm went off. She decided to break with tradition and call him for a change. The phone rang six times before going to voicemail. She hung up and decided he would see her number and return her call. When he had not called back in thirty minutes, she tried again. This time he answered on the third ring.

"Good morning, Beautiful," he said sleepily. "What time is it?"

"A quarter to six," she responded, grateful to hear his voice.

"Is everything okay?" he asked as he started to clear his foggy head.

"Yes, I just wanted to catch you in the shower for once," she said trying to hide a giggle in her voice. "I couldn't stop thinking about you and would like to break a few ground rules. Instead of going out this weekend, I want you to come over here and let me cook for you."

Her mother had been an awesome cook and had taught her all she knew. Sonja, her mother, had loved cooking and so had her mother, Ashley's grandmother, and her mother before that. Cooking had become a family tradition in Ashley's family and the recipes were passed down for generations. Sonja's specialty had always been lasagna. Her great aunt had passed the recipe down to her when she came over from Italy. This, too, was Ashley's go-to favorite, and she had never had any complaints.

Her mother was overjoyed when Ashley told her Mark had proposed in the second semester of their junior year. She advised her daughter not to rush into it until after her learning was completed. They set a date of July 23rd the next year. After they graduated, they married and then her life changed.

That first night, they gave themselves to each other for the first time. They got little sleep, but had a lot of laughs and made love three times. The next morning, they both turned their cell phones back on and Ashley saw she had several missed calls from Garry. He had not left a voicemail. She remembered how thankful she had been the previous day since he had been able to give her away, and how dashing he looked in his good suit. She returned his call.

"Garry, the honeymoon is going great. Do you miss me already?" she asked in a playful tone.

"Ash, I have some bad news. When your mother was leaving the reception last night, she was broadsided by a drunk driver. She was taken to the hospital, but passed away in route," he said breaking down. "Your mother is gone."

Garry died a year later of a heart attack. A year to the day.

Tim agreed to be at her house by 7 p.m. and said he would bring the wine. They got off the phone, and she started her day with a bath, as usual. The week seemed to drag on for both of them, everyday getting longer and longer until finally it was Thursday night. She decided to take Friday off, so she could make the dinner plans, get the groceries, and prepare herself for the next step. She was nervous all day in anticipation of sharing the house, but the day seemed to fly by. As she was pulling the lasagna out of the oven, her doorbell rang. She could see it was a tall handsome man, about six-foot, with coal-black hair under his Stetson cowboy hat. He was dressed in a black suit and was holding a bouquet in his right hand. As she opened the door, she leaned in for a kiss.

He didn't know what to expect that night, but was ready for anything she could throw at him. All she had said was it was going to be a quiet evening, dinner, and they could get comfortable on the couch and watch a movie on the big screen. It turned out to be a romantic movie, although neither one of them was able to see much due to the kissing and caressing they did. As the credits rolled, she broke the ice by telling him she was falling in love with him. She hadn't felt this way about anyone else except Mark.

"You loved him very much, didn't you?" he asked.

She nodded with a tear in her eye and said, "He was a lot like you. A true gentleman, strong, and caring. I feel like I am cheating on him when I am with you. I loved him so much and now he is gone."

"I didn't know him as well or as long as you, but I know he would want you to be happy. I only met him in our senior year of college. When I moved out here for my job and education. He was a great friend and introduced me to so many people, including you. I miss him a lot as well." He whispered as he held her against his chest, "You have to move on with your life. You have to realize this is a new chapter."

He took her by the hand and led her upstairs to her bedroom. Laying her on the bed, he kissed her one more time before telling her to get some sleep. He knew she had drunk a little too much wine that night and showed himself to the door, locking it as he closed it behind himself.

The next morning, she was awakened to her phone ringing. He was calling to check up on her. The ringing continued through the entire phone call and as she hung up, she realized it was just another hangover.

"What happened last night? All I can remember is moving to the couch and now waking up in bed. Did anything happen. . . Did we. . .?" she asked in a panicked tone.

He explained he had remained a gentleman, and that her honor was still intact. He also explained it was one of the hardest things he had ever done and told her he loved her for the first time. She invited him over again that day, and he accepted with the stipulation the next date had to be at his place. She agreed.

He arrived at her house around noon. They went into town for lunch at Rusty's Restaurant and then to the park. Holding hands, he recapped the previous evening as they walked in the spring air. The flowers were blooming and the world felt right. They made plans for the next weekend's date night to be at his home, and he would pick her up at 6:30 p.m. on Friday night.

That week flew by as he prepared for her visit. He was busier than normal at work and did not get everything set up the way he wanted for the date. Then, Friday came. They had already taken vacation time for the next 10 days and would try to spend it with each other as much as possible. That night he made steak and baked potatoes for dinner. He knew it was one of her favorites. The steak was cooked to a perfect medium rare and the potatoes had all the fixings. After dinner, he put on some slow, romantic music, took her by the hand, and asked her to dance. As they danced, she seemed to slip into his arms tighter and tighter. After a few slow songs he sat her on his love seat, knelt before her and proposed. She immediately began to cry, hiding her face in his chest. She said yes. That is when he woke up Friday at 6 a.m. as usual.

"A dream. . . that's all it was. Just a damn dream," he spoke in anger. "Soon I will make it become reality." He muttered as he glanced at the little jewelry box next to his bed.

He did have a date with Ashley that night at his place. He had started a two-week vacation that day, and he knew he loved her. The rest had been so vivid and felt right. He couldn't believe it was just a dream.

He grabbed his phone and called her. She was already in the bath and ready for the call. They talked for a few minutes and confirmed he would pick her up at 6:30 p.m.. As they got off the phone call, he looked around and thought about all the stuff he had to do to get ready for her visit. Before getting out of bed, he looked at the ring box one more time and knew she was not ready yet. With a sigh, he placed it into his bedside drawer.

Dinner went as planned. Like in his dream, they ate, danced, and snuggled on the love seat, but that is where the similarities ended. He drove her home that night about 11:00 p.m. He walked her to the door, kissed her, and told her again he loved her. She blushed and turned away. As she entered her humble abode, she told him to call her when he got home, just to make sure he was safe. As she heard his truck leaving, she leaned against the door and whispered that she, too, loved him. This was the first time she had consciously allowed herself to forget about Mark. She knew he would make a great husband. That night she told him out loud she loved him and quickly blushed again.

She felt like a school girl with her first crush, all tingly inside. She then curled up in her favorite blanket and drifted off to sleep. She dreamed about him as usual that night. She dreamt he was kissing her, allowing his hands to slowly caress her back. He then caressed her naked stomach up to her breast as he laid her on the bed. She dreamt they were about to make love when she was awakened by the ringing of her alarm clock.

Then came July. The second hardest month for Ashley. As the month progressed, so did her depression. She loved and missed her mother. She spent the whole day of the 23rd at Tim's place, in his arms, crying on his shoulder. She hardly ate anything, but they talked about the loss of her parents and Mark. Tim had gone to Mark's funeral and consoled her there. Her dad had suggested Ashley, Tim, and Sarah go for coffee and talk, remembering the man Mark had been.

Over coffee, they exchanged numbers, and he had told her he would do anything, anytime she needed it. A week later, she called him and asked him to meet up somewhere for a little companionship. She was lost without Mark. That went on for a while, and then they officially started dating. Their first date was awkward. She had cried and kept calling him by her late husband's name. Each date got a little easier for her as she got more and more comfortable with Tim. Each time they went out, she felt like she was cheating on Mark.

That night, she drank wine to try to numb herself, as did he. His heart was breaking seeing her in this pain. As the night rolled on and the bottles emptied, he suggested she stay the night. They both had too much to drink to be driving; for their safety, she agreed. He made up the bed in the second bedroom and led her to the room. With a kiss goodnight and the promise he would not leave her, she drifted off to sleep. After watching her sleep for about a half an hour, he got up from the lounge chair and retired to his room. Saturday morning, she awoke to find him sitting in the same chair.

"Have you been there all night?" she asked surprise.

"No, I came in about five minutes ago," he said as he kissed her good morning. After breakfast, they sat around and talked.

That was twice he had gotten her in bed, and nothing happened either time. Twice he had been a total gentleman and not taken advantage of her. "That was twice," she thought to herself, "he could have had sex with me, but he didn't even try. Twice I would not have resisted. Damn, he's a gentleman!"

It was more than twice she had wanted him to make a move, but she had laid down ground rules on their first date; no sex until marriage, no going to the other's house, and no kissing until the third date. She had already broken two of the three and was longing for the third. She actually kissed him on the second date. It was just a little peck goodnight, but it was still a small kiss. She did not know how much longer she could keep the third rule. Every time he looked at her, she felt warm and fuzzy inside. He turned her on every time he touched her. She had strong urges to make love to him.

They called it a day around 10 p.m., and he drove her home. The next few months went like all the rest with only one exception. They visited each other's place more frequently. By the time September arrived, they were seeing each other's homes every other weekend. Occasionally, she would sleep over at his place, but nothing ever happened, and he never stayed at hers.

In September, she had an idea and invited him over. She told him to not bring any wine, but instead to bring some giant marshmallows, wear jeans, and dress down, informing him that tonight they would have a quiet and relaxing date. This, of course, raised his curiosity, but he did as requested. When he arrived at her house, she was waiting for him at the door.

"It took you long enough to get here," she spoke through a smile.

"It is an hour from town and the deer are running rampant," he said laughing back.

She was dressed in jeans he swore had to have been sewn on and a white cotton T-shirt that emphasized her breasts. She was holding two large bags and two wire sticks. He was dressed in jeans and a shirt he had obviously had since college. He was holding the marshmallows she had requested in one hand and a dozen roses in the other. She took the flowers, putting them in a vase, while telling him to follow her. They went through the kitchen and out the backdoor. After a few minutes' walk down the path, he saw the campsite as they emerged through the woods. He saw the lit fire down by the pond in the early twilight, a tent, a picnic basket, and a large downed tree for them to sit on.

"Tonight, our date is going to be out here," she said slyly, "under the stars."

The night was beautiful, all the stars were out. The fire kept them warm throughout the evening. They talked about nothing, ate, and cuddled by the fire. They roasted marshmallows, feeding them to each other. The night cooled down as they let the fire die. Around midnight, she turned to him, informing him that it was time for bed. He rose first and immediately knelt before her.

"I have been holding on to something for about a year now and thought it might be a good time to give it to you," he said as he held an engagement ring in front of her. "Ashley Renee Brown, will you make me the happiest man in the world. Will you marry me?"

"Yes," she said as the tears of joy slowly ran down her cheeks.

They were going to sleep together in the tent in separate sleeping bags. That was until he suggested they lay on one and cover themselves with the other. She smiled at the idea of sharing a bed with him, her husband-to-be, and agreed.

They snuggled in the tent, kissing each other for another hour or so, then fell asleep in each other's arms.

He awoke the next morning to the smell of fish frying. Ashley had already caught and cleaned breakfast, built a fire, and started cooking. He knew she was an early riser, but not an overachiever. He told her this as he walked up behind her to give her a kiss.

"Last night was magical," he spoke as he ate the bass. "I haven't been camping since I was a child in the Boy Scouts. Where did you learn to do all this?"

"Girl Scouts. And Garry," she said sheepishly.

"Well, I loved it and I love you," he spoke.

"I love you too, Tim. I really do," she said with a catch in her voice.

After breakfast, they packed up the campsite, making sure the fire was out, and headed for the house. Once inside the house, they put the sleeping bags and tent into the storage room.

"I need to go home and clean up; I still have marshmallows on my shirt and I think I need a nap. I will see you tonight. How about 6 p.m. at my place?" he said sleepily.

"That sounds good. I think I will get a nap in as well," she spoke through a yawn.

They kissed one more time before Tim headed for his truck and left. It was only 7:30 p.m., but she knew she had to call Sarah, as she had after each of their dates. She had to make sure Sarah would be okay with everything. She wanted to make sure Mark would have been okay with the current situation.

"Sarah, I have to talk to you. Can I come over? It's kind of important," Ashley stated as soon as Sarah answered the phone.

"Sure, are you at your house or at Tim's?" Sarah asked knowing that she was probably at Tim's. She knew that Ashley had been spending the night over there and assumed she had last night.

"Mine," Ashley responded to Sarah's surprise. "It will take me about an hour and a half to get there. I need to shower first."

"Come on over. I'll see you when you get here," Sarah said with a joyful tone in her voice. Sarah always loved seeing Ashley and treasured their friendship. It had been almost two weeks since they had seen each other. The last time had been at Ashley's place. Sarah had brought Brandon, her son, over to see his Aunt Ashley.

"He is getting big," Ashley had stated, and he was. Over the last three years, he had grown from a tiny baby to the curious child he now was.

Ashley loved Brandon and he loved his aunt. As they played, he would giggle, making Ashley laugh.

This morning, Ashley just took a fast shower instead of her normal bath. She dressed conservatively and headed towards town. When Ashley arrived at Sarah's house, she was met by Brandon. He came running out of the front door as she pulled into the driveway. He gave her a big hug and a kiss on the cheek. As they entered the house, Sarah asked Brandon to go to his room while they talked.

Ashley recounted the previous night's events, and waited for Sarah's response. She had prepared herself for everything on the hour ride over. As Ashley got to the proposal and showed the ring, Sarah began to cry.

"It's about time he asked," Sarah said in a gleeful tone as she hugged Ashley. "Congratulations. I assume you said yes."

They talked for about an hour and Sarah reassured Ashley Mark would want this, telling Ashley that she knew all Mark had ever wanted was for her to be happy. After a few more hugs, Ashley left saying she needed to get home and get ready for the night. With her worst fears vanquished, she drove home for a light lunch and a much-needed nap.

She got to Tim's at 5:45 p.m., parked in the garage, and sat in her car for 15 minutes trying to calm herself for the date. She was so nervous and scared that she would break her last rule. She finally decided if it happens then it happens. She was a grown woman; she could sleep with Tim if she wanted to, and she did want to. Upon reaching his apartment door, she had decided tonight was the night she would give herself to him completely. She was actually turned on about the decision when she knocked. He answered the door and greeted her with a kiss.

"Something smells good," she stated.

"I am making us a couple of steaks and baked potatoes for dinner. They should be ready in about five minutes," he said with a smile.

They ate dinner and talked about whom they had told the good news to. Ashley told him about her trip to Sarah's and how happy she had been. After dinner, they sat on the love seat to watch a movie. She snuggled close to him, and he covered them with a blanket. About 10 minutes into the movie, she laid her head on his shoulder and drifted off to sleep. After the movie he picked her up and took her to the spare bedroom, placing her gently on the bed and tucked her in for the night. With a light kiss he let her sleep.

The next morning, she awoke at 5 a.m. with disappointment in her heart. She couldn't believe nothing had happened again. She got out of bed and went into his room, waking him with a kiss. She kept her disappointment to herself as they made breakfast and ate. Around 9 a.m., she left for her house, so she could get ready for the work week ahead.

When she got home, she called Sarah again, asking her to help plan the wedding and to be her maid of honor. Sarah was delighted with this offer and accepted right away and informed her the wedding would be paid for in total by her. Ashley informed her they were thinking of a spring wedding sometime in May.

Over the next few months, all three of them decided the best place to have the wedding would be by the pond at Ashley's house. There would be plenty of room for all the guests. Tim thought this was especially a good idea, knowing that this was a way for Mark to still be at the wedding.

"I want you to stay the weekend at my place, next weekend," she said knowing what that might mean.

She had spent the week excited and as the weekend approached, she got more and more turned on. She was downright horny when he arrived at her house Friday night at 6:30 p.m. He brought an overnight bag and a pillow, not exactly sure what to expect. Like usual, they ate dinner and watched a movie on the big screen. They cuddled on the couch and made out throughout the evening. When it was time for bed, she told him to grab his bag and showed him to his room, hoping he would balk at the idea. His room was large with a queen-sized bed. His room had an en suite in which she had placed fresh towels that afternoon. They both longed to share the same bed, but neither would break the rule.

She awoke at 5 a.m. the next morning, took her normal hour long bath, dressed, and headed towards the kitchen to make them breakfast. She had the coffee ready and the pancakes were almost done when Tim walked in.

"Good morning handsome, how did you sleep?" she asked while flipping the last pancake.

"It would have been better if you were in bed with me, but then I probably would not have slept at all," he spoke through a yawn.

"I know what you mean, and you are a bad boy for talking that way so early in the morning," she scolded him jokingly as she kissed him. "Maybe I should just spank you."

"Yes, please do, I am a bad boy," he laughed as he returned the kiss.

Tim and Ashley still saw each other on the weekends. Sometimes she would sleep over at Tim's place, always hoping he would make the first move. He never did and she always took the second bedroom. The only thing that really changed was the fact that Tim started sleeping in one of the extra bedrooms at her house. The first time he did this, he felt awkward and wanted to make the first move but always remembered the ground rules.

Ashley spent a lot of time at Sarah's house the next few months, and learned more about her family as they planned the wedding. They'd spent so much time together that Ashley decided to quit her job so she could focus on the task at hand. Sarah enjoyed the company and Brandon loved seeing his Aunt Ashley damn near every day.

Sarah had remained single during her pregnancy with Brandon. The one-night stand never called her again. She had decided she would raise her child alone. She had planned on having her brother Mark be the "man" in Brandon's life but that dream was cut short. She could not get help from her parents since they had died when she was a child. Her aunts and uncles helped raise the two children since Sarah and Mark were both 10 years old at the time of their parents' demise.

When they turned eighteen, the college of their choice was paid for in full by the trust their parents had set up in case of an emergency. The day they turned 21, the trust released another $21 million to each of them. The remainder would be issued to them upon their 30th birthday, for a grand total of $100 million each. Since Mark had died before he reached this age, the trust gave it to his widow, setting Ashley up for life.

Sarah's aunts and uncles loved Brandon and had already set up a trust for him. They also spoiled the shit out of him. His great-aunt Martha was so wrapped around his little finger. The family all agreed that he looked like his uncle Mark. At three, he was already reading and doing simple addition problems like his uncle, and they knew he was highly intelligent. Sarah had him in daycare throughout the mornings and had a private tutor for him three days a week. He loved to learn; she knew he would become a doctor or lawyer someday. He also loved to play and was given every opportunity to do so. He was not forced to learn, although he enjoyed it. When Brandon had been two, he had already begun to read "Dick and Jane" by himself, his favorite book, sounding out some words and asking for help on others. He was a child prodigy, and everyone who knew him knew he would go far.

Sarah had two uncles and one aunt on her father's side and one uncle and aunt on her mother's. Aunt Martha was her mother's sister and had been closest to Sarah as she grew up, being the primary adult in their lives. She had never married and had no children of her own, although, Sarah and Mark thought she was a great mother.

Ashley had talked to Sarah one day about quitting her job. Sarah had explained that the money she had gotten from the trust was okay to live on. The family had given it to her to do with as she wanted. She did not have to work. The next day she gave her two weeks' notice.

Sarah also talked to her about getting a wedding dress. Ashley did not want to wear the one she had worn for Mark.

"When you come over tomorrow, we will go to a tailor and pick something that will be beautiful and stunning," Sarah stated in a matter-of-fact tone.

The next day, they looked at hundreds of dress designs and agreed on one. It was a strapless dress, crafted in soft tulle and delicate layers of lace petals that fluttered about the sweetheart bodice and floated down an elegant princess skirt. Ashley asked to get it in an Ivory color. She felt white would be a lie since she was not a virgin. She had been married to a wonderful man, whom she loved and always would. She did not want to disrespect that side of the family, or her beloved Mark. The tailor took her measurements and they ordered the dress.

That night she called Tim and told him about quitting her job, and that they had found a dress and it would be ready some time in December. They talked for about an hour about the previous days' events and how much they loved each other. As they chatted, she explained Mark's family would be at the wedding, and Tim loved the idea. He had met Sarah a couple of times and liked her. He thought she was a great friend and an even better mother. He and Ashley had taken Brandon to the zoo over the summer, and he thought Brandon was a wonderful kid. He hoped to have a child half as good as Brandon one day and told Ashley so many times since. As the got off the phone, he told her again he loved her and sent her a kiss.

The next day, as Tim was getting ready for work, someone knocked on his door. It was Ashley holding a caramel macchiato. She was wearing a pink chiffon blouse and a tight black miniskirt.

"This is a surprise," he stated as she handed him the drink.

"I have another surprise for you," she said with a smile. "May I come in?"

"Of course," he said, "Mi casa es su casa."

"I am glad you feel that way," she said as she sat on his loveseat. "I feel the same way and have decided to give you this," handing him a key to her house. "Now you can come and go whenever you want. And if you want to start 'accidentally' leaving clothing or stuff there, that would be okay, too."

She was trying to make the first move, hoping it would lead to the breaking of the third rule. He knew what this meant and fought hard to suppress the urge to take her to his room. Looking at the clock, he saw he needed to leave for work or else he would be late. He informed her of this and told her she could stay as long as she wanted. He would get a key for her and drop it by her house that evening.

While sitting on her couch that day, she felt discouraged. She had wanted to give him another gift that morning, but he must not have gotten the message, she thought. She was ready to break her third rule, but instead curled up with her special blanket and fell asleep right there on the couch.

He came over at 6:30 p.m. as promised with her key to his place. Even though it was a weekday, they had a date. After dinner, she told him she wanted to talk to him about something serious. As they sat on the couch, she recounted the three rules and how she had been the one to break the first two. She told him she was ready to break the third and asked him if he was willing to do so that night.

"Honey, I love you and respect your urges. I too, would like to make love with you, but I don't think the timing is right tonight. I had a hard day at work and I want to be able to give you my complete best. Besides that, I don't think Mark would want you to give yourself away, out of wedlock. I am sorry but I think we should wait the next few months until our wedding." He said nervously.

They talked about their feelings for each other well into the night. At 1:15 a.m., he finally said he would head home. She objected and told him he was being silly. He would sleep in the guest room he had stayed in before. She knew he woke about 6 a.m. and promised she would get him up.

"You already have," he stated as they headed to their rooms and said their goodnights. She blushed at the thought and kissed him.

"You're being dirty. . . I thought we just talked about that," she said through a stifled laugh.

Even though they had agreed to wait, the desire in her groin was running rampant. That night, she satisfied herself with him sleeping in the next room.

The next morning, she woke him as promised by climbing into the opposite side of the bed and giving him a kiss and a hug.

"You don't really need to go to work today, do you?" she pleaded. "You could take the day off and spend it with me." She gently began to rub his chest.

"Okay, I will call in sick today," he said as they began to wrestle on the bed.

Knowing that he was a senior distribution manager at the delivery hub he worked at, she knew he had a little extra freedom to take time off. He had been transferred there from Texas four and a half years ago. He had actually began working for the headquarters when he was sixteen and quickly moved up in the ranks. He started as a line man and worked his way up to manager until the summer between his junior and senior years in college. He was offered a promotion to senior manager of distribution affairs but had to move north. After some time of thinking and talking to his parents about it, he accepted the offer. He now knew that it had been his best move ever.

Laying there in bed with her made him want her even more, but his will was good, for now at least. He kissed her again, grabbed his phone, and made the call. After he hung up his cell phone, he rolled over and playfully attacked Ashley, pinning her to the bed and tickling her. She, in turn, started tickling him back. They both were laughing when her stomach began to growl. She decided to make breakfast for them both.

After breakfast, they took a walk down to the pond and fished for a couple of hours. They caught and released six fish. Although Tim swore she was cheating somehow, she'd caught four of them and he told her two of them were the same fish. After fishing, they walked around the woods hand-in-hand, discussing their future living arrangements. They decided that since his lease would be up at the end of January that he would just move in then. Her house had plenty of room for his stuff, and she relished the idea of having a man in the house. After lunch, they both went to see Sarah and Brandon.

They informed Sarah of their decision, and she thought it was a good thing, too. Tim and Brandon got along great and loved to play together. Brandon started calling him Uncle Tim and this made Tim's heart swell. Sarah saw how they played together and told Ashley that she thought Tim was going to be a great father one day. This made Ashley blush, and she recounted the previous evening's discussion. Sarah had mixed feelings on the subject. Being a single mother, she had sex out of wedlock and understood the urges. She also respected Ashley's decision to wait, both for herself and for Mark.

"This must be driving Tim nuts," Sarah stated.

"He is taking it very well; I have made the first move several times, and he still has not gone there," Ashley said a little begrudgingly.

"You really want to do it, don't you?" Sarah asked quietly, so that the boys could not hear, already knowing the answer.

Over the last seven years of knowing each other, the two ladies had become like sisters and could talk openly about anything, and usually did. Ashley knew about the dates Sarah went on, and Sarah knew about the dates between Ashley and Tim. Ashley also knew that Sarah for the most part was not waiting for marriage to have sex, but rarely had sex on the first date. Ashley informed her about touching herself last night and how she felt guilty and aroused with him in the next room. She also told Sarah that it was getting harder and harder ever day to abstain from sex and masturbation. That's when the boys came close again and the conversation changed.

They stayed at Sarah's throughout the early evening, then Tim decided to take them all out for dinner. They decided to go to Rusty's Restaurant where the adults had steaks and Brandon had a chicken nugget meal with mac and cheese. They talked as they ate and Sarah told Tim that they needed to get together sometime. Just the two of them. Ashley thought this was a great idea and encouraged him to call her that weekend. Instead, they made plans to get together right there over dinner. Tim would meet Sarah at Rusty's around 6 p.m. on Friday, and they could have dinner and a conversation.

"Now, don't go forgetting about me on your date," Ashley said with a laugh.

"Don't worry, honey, I could never forget about you," Tim said as he kissed her.

After dinner, they returned to Sarah's home and said their goodbyes. Brandon was almost asleep when they got home, and Tim asked if he could put him to bed. Sarah agreed, showing him to Brandon's room, watching as he gently placed him in bed and gave him a goodnight kiss.

"I'll see you soon, buddy," he said as he lightly walked out of the room.

"You are going to be a great father someday," Sarah softly said to him.

They all took turns hugging and then Ashley and Tim left. The night was still young, and they were not ready to go home yet. They decided to go for coffee and talk for a while. A couple of hours later, Tim looked at his watch and realized it was almost ten o'clock at night. They decided Tim would drop her off at home and return to his apartment. He would call her when he got home as usual.

When he called her that night, Ashley told him she appreciated all that he had done with Brandon. Tim stated he had enjoyed the time spent at Sarah's playing with Brandon. She also told him that night he would make a great father someday. They talked for about 30 minutes, and she tried to talk him into calling in sick again the next day, but to no avail. The weekend was coming, and he would see both ladies then.

His time with Sarah went well. She had gotten a sitter for Brandon and had actually beaten him to the restaurant by 15 minutes. She had already gotten a table near the door so she could see him when he entered and drank a beer. She was a little nervous meeting and did not want to, in any way, make him think she was hitting on him. She loved Ashley too much for any drama there.

"You look nice, Sarah," he said as he entered.

"Thank you but it's just jeans and a t-shirt," she said as she finished her second beer.

Over dinner, he felt like she was almost interrogating him. During that conversation, she asked Tim about his family, work, friends, and his feelings for Ashley, all of which she pretty much knew, having been told by Ashley already. She was playing the protective big sister role, even though Ashley was two months older and he knew it. He let her question him and waited for his turn, but it never came. After dinner, they moved to the bar and had a couple of drinks as the interrogation continued. He could sense she was starting to flirt with him more and more. When she put her hand on his leg, he brushed it off saying he had to go. He stated Ashley would be expecting him home any time now and informing her that it was an hour drive to her house. They hugged gently and parted ways. Sarah knew Tim would not drive while on his phone and took that drive time to call Ashley and inform her of how their plan had gone.

"He was a perfect gentleman," Sarah told Ashley after the fifteen minute drive home. "I did as you asked, made every pass I could think of, short of flat out asking him to fuck me, and he would not bite. He does love you very much and would not cheat on you. I truly believe this."

They talked for a while about everything that had happened that night until Ashley heard Tim's truck pulling into her driveway. They quickly got off the phone just as Tim entered the house. He seemed a little upset when she asked him how the evening went. He told her what she already knew, but through his eyes. He explained how she hit on him and said he did not trust her that much anymore. He explained how uncomfortable he had felt and how much he loved Ashley.

At this point, Ashley confessed it was a test to see if he would have sex with just anyone, or if he was true to her. She also informed him that Sarah had not wanted to go through with it but had been convinced to do so by her over the last part of the week. She explained the conversation they had earlier that week made her question her rule about no sex until marriage. She said she trusted him, but had to find out for sure. She then told him about what she had done the last time he spent the night, explaining how hard he makes abstinence. She asked him to forgive her for the deception and Sarah, too. He agreed now that he understood the situation fully.

That night she slept poorly knowing how she had upset him. She had promised him it would never happen again as they both headed to their own rooms. When she awoke, he was sitting in the chair beside her bed.

"How long do you plan to sit there?" she asked slightly startling him.

"I couldn't sleep, I kept thinking about Sarah, how much y'all care about each other and me," he spoke in a softened tone. "What would you have done if I had slept with her?"

"It never would have gone that far. She would have stopped you after a kiss," she responded to his question with certainty.

"I have to go think about this. I will call you when I am ready to talk." He said with distress in his voice.

He stood and exited her room, telling her that he loved her as he left. She cried herself to sleep that night. In the morning, she waited for his call, but it never came. Around noon, she called Sarah and informed her of the current situation. Sarah was as upset with the turn of events as was Ashley. She asked if Ashley could use some company and got a heavy sob as a response as Ashley broke down crying again. They got off the phone; Sarah and Brandon made their way to Ashley's house. She took overnight bags with them and knew she had a room at Ashley's for as long as she needed her to be there. Sarah made the trip in only 45 minutes and was met at the door by a sobbing Ashley. The two of them talked about what to do while Brandon played in his playroom at Aunt Ashley's.

Over the next few days, Sarah stayed to keep Ashley company, leaving only to take Brandon to daycare. Ashley usually rode with her to pick him up and Brandon loved seeing his aunt daily. On Wednesday, Ashley almost called Tim but could not hit send on her cell phone. By Friday, she was going nuts. That night around 6:30 p.m. came a knock on her door. It was Tim. He said he knew Sarah was over there because her car was in the driveway, and he was glad because he felt they all needed to talk.

"This has been the hardest week I have ever had," he started the conversation off. He then vented to Ashley and Sarah both, talking for almost two hours. They sat quietly letting him clear the air, only talking to answer his direct questions. He never raised his voice, but they knew he was very upset still. After he said his peace, before they could say anything, he stated that he was going to leave, telling Ashley that he still loved her but still needed more time to think. He left just as he had come—quickly.

Sarah continued to stay at Ashley's house for the next week. On Saturday morning, Tim called Ashley, asking her to please come to his apartment for dinner. She arrived at his apartment building around 5:30 p.m. and tried to regain her composure. She had thought about the events that had unfolded over the last two weeks and was not sure if Tim would forgive her and Sarah while on the hour drive. She sat for the next half hour, steadying herself for the worst yet hoping for the best. At 6 p.m., she knocked on his door, hoping he would not notice she was so scared; she was shaking. When he opened the door, she saw the table had been set with fresh flowers and lit candles. She knew this could go one of two ways and entered his apartment.

"I have made Fettuccine Alfredo for dinner; I hope you don't mind Italian tonight," he said as he kissed her. "Tonight, we eat in peace then afterwards, we will talk about the situation at hand," he said as he led her to the table.

The conversation at dinner included a lot of small talk about his work and even more apologies from her. Each time she tried to apologize, he would cut her off and tell her that was for after dinner talk. She could see he was still upset and did not want to hurt him anymore. After dinner, they retired to the love seat in his living room. He made coffee for them, and she sat beside him as he started talking.

"This whole thing has upset me; in case you couldn't tell. I have been respectful of your wishes or rules or whatever you want to call them and I have not broken one. You, on the other hand, broke them almost right away. I remember our second date when you kissed me. I remember being surprised by that. Even more surprised, when you asked me over to your place for the first time. I was even surprised when we went camping and slept in the same tent. I have never given you any reason not to trust me, but yet you had to test me. You talked Sarah into going against her best judgment and got her to help you try to see if I would cheat. I understand you were feeling guilty about what you did the night I slept over at your house, but you don't need to. We all have urges and I have done the same thing a time or two thinking of you. I understand sex before marriage would be a dishonor to Mark and his memory and have accepted that I will have to wait. If it would make you feel better about me and the fact I do love you so much, then let's go into my room and fuck. I don't want to just fuck someone. I want to make love to you and you alone. I want to make love to you as my wife. I respect your urges as you must respect mine, but I have not ever looked elsewhere for satisfaction of them, nor would I." He rose off the love seat.

"I asked you to marry me, because I loved you and still do very much. I just need to know that you trust me and this is not the way to show it. I thought we were growing closer, then you tried to drive us apart. Is that what you want? Your freedom? If so, I will back out of your life, no matter how I feel about you. But I love you and still want to be married to you and you alone."

When he paused to take a drink of the coffee, she spoke softly and shyly.

"I do trust you and do want to marry you, I am sorry for upsetting you and I hope we can get back to where we were before I screwed up," she said as she too rose from the love seat. "If you will forgive me then I would be willing to break the last rule, if you want. I want to give myself to you completely tonight, so tomorrow I will know that you still are happy with me," she said with tears in her eyes. "I love you Tim, more than I have ever loved anyone else, even Mark. I was just scared of losing you, because of my stupid rules."

He turned to her and took her into his arms, holding her tight. They kissed for what seemed like a long time until she broke away asking if it meant she had been forgiven. He responded in the affirmative and kissed her again. They sat back down and discussed how they would treat each other from that point on. He knew he had to apologize to Sarah and told Ashley. Ashley called Sarah and found out she was still at her house. Ashley asked Sarah to stay the night again that night and informed her they would be there as soon as they could. Ashley left her car in Tim's parking garage that night and rode back to her house with him.

Sarah was sitting on the couch when they arrived and looked very nervous. She hadn't seen Tim since the previous weekend when he lectured them on their little stunt. She did not know what happened over dinner and expected to get ripped into again by Tim. He saw the uncertainty in her eyes as he walked in the house and quickly started to discuss his feelings to her. After he finished, she too asked for forgiveness for her role in the fiasco, reassuring him that it would never happen again. Then they hugged and she kissed him on the cheek.

"I would like to get to know you better," she spoke. "Especially if the wedding is still on. It is still on, isn't it?"

"Yes, it is," they both said in unison.

# Chapter 2

Brandon had been in bed asleep the night before and did not know his uncle Tim was coming over. When he found out in the morning, he ran to Tim's room and woke him up. Tim awoke to Brandon jumping onto his bed. The action brought a smile directly to Tim's face. As he laughed out loud, Sarah entered his room scolding Brandon for waking Tim.

"Well, hello there. What time is it?" Tim asked.

"It is a quarter to nine," she replied. "I am so sorry for this. He got excited to see you. I am sorry he woke you up."

"If that's the worst thing that happens today. . .," he started to say when Brandon hugged him, interrupting his thought process.

"You seemed like you were tired, so I convinced Ashley to let you sleep," Sarah said, hoping he was not upset as Ashley walked up beside her.

"Good morning, handsome," Ashley said as she entered the room to give him a kiss. "Breakfast is downstairs, if you are hungry."

They kissed with Brandon still hugging his beloved uncle. After cleaning up, Tim went downstairs and grabbed some breakfast, sausage, eggs, and toast. He told the ladies he was sorry for the way he handled everything over the last two weeks and that if they could put it all behind them, he would appreciate it. They spent that morning walking through the woods and around the pond. Tim and Ashley took turns holding Brandon's little hand along with each other's.

"How did you ever get such a wonderful man like Tim?" Sarah asked as they returned to the house around noon.

"I set up the ground rules on the first date and expected him to follow them." Ashley replied.

The ladies sat around that afternoon talking as Tim and Brandon played. Sarah wanted some advice on dating and Ashley gladly gave it to her. Sarah advised her she wanted to find a man as nice and sweet as she had. One that would not find out about Brandon, then turn and run. She wanted to settle down and eventually get married as well.

Over the next few hours, Ashley and Sarah made plans for Ashley's wedding and for the next man Sarah would date. Sarah understood the three little rules, but didn't think she could follow them. Ashley advised her it was okay to break the first rule, but that the other two need to take some time before breaking. The rules were simple. One, do not kiss until the third date. Two, always meet in public, never at each other's house. Three, do not have sex until marriage. Ashley knew this last one was the hardest to follow, but also knew that if Sarah would try to keep it, she would find the right guy. Ashley also told her to be honest about Brandon on the first date.

Ashley told Sarah to do like she had done, and let her know how the dates go, in detail, not to leave anything out, and she would help her through the hard times. Sarah agreed. Sarah informed her there was a guy that had asked her out for the following Friday night and asked if they could double date that night. It was supposed to be dinner at Rusty's at 6 p.m. and maybe drinks afterword. She also informed her that Brandon would be staying with his great-aunt Martha for the weekend. Ashley told her it would be fine with her and would let Tim know of their new date. At 5:30 p.m. Sarah and Brandon left to get ready for the week ahead and to give Ashley and Tim some alone time. That week flew by. Ashley had found a caterer and ordered the flowers; Tim had got the airline tickets for his parents.

Sarah had let her date know about the three rules and Ashley and Tim would be joining them for dinner. She also informed him about Brandon telling him they would not meet until the time was right. She thought five or six dates would be enough for him to meet the most important man in her life. Especially since most of her dates had never run past date number two. She usually slept with them on the first or second date then they were gone out of her life. She had dated frequently, about twice a month, but rarely with the same guy. She admitted she was starting to feel like a slut to Ashley on one of their phone calls that week. Ashley had stated they would change that.

Tim stayed at his apartment that week seeing Ashley only a couple of times before their Friday night date. Every morning he would call her at 6 p.m. as she took her bath, then again in the evenings. They talked about the upcoming date and Tim found out the man in question was named Dave. Sarah had met him at the gym, and he had a nice smile. That was about all she knew for sure; all Sarah had told her.

When Friday came around, Ashley dressed in her green dress that she had worn on a previous date with Tim and high heels. This time she had her hair in a pony tail. She drove to Tim's apartment and was waiting on the love seat for him, when he got home from work. This was the first time she had used the key he had given her. When he entered the apartment, he was happy to see her, kissed her and told her he needed to get ready for their date. He asked her to wait in the living room while he took a quick shower and got dressed.

"No peeking," he said jokingly as he headed for his bedroom.

Thirty minutes later, he came out wearing a black suit, cowboy boots, and his favorite Stetson cowboy hat. They met Sarah at the restaurant 15 minutes before her date. She was dressed in a light pink blouse and a black skirt that stopped halfway to her knees. Her brown hair was in a ponytail like Ashley's. Sarah gave a little more information about Dave that night while they waited on him to show. He arrived five minutes early and saw Sarah right away.

Over dinner, the conversation flowed and everyone enjoyed themselves. Dave wanted to see photos of Brandon and both ladies pulled out their phones. As the evening wound down, he asked for a second date next weekend, and she accepted. After he left the restaurant, the three of them decided to go to Sarah's house to talk about their date.

Ashley told them Dave was a nice-looking man, witty, and charming, but would not say that she did not think he was right for her. She held on to that opinion just to see where things went. She would later that night tell Tim, but only when they were alone at his apartment. Dave had informed them he had just passed the bar in the last month and would be starting his own law firm at the beginning of the new year. He had already gotten the lease signed and was to move into the office space January 1st. Until then, he was taking some time off to recoup from the stress of taking the test. He also informed them it had taken him three tries to pass.

Something did not sit right with Ashley about Dave, and she told Tim this that night. He seemed a little too eager to accept the rules and a little forced when he answered their questions.

"He was nervous. There he was with two people he had never met, trying to impress Sarah," Tim had stated when she elaborated on the date.

"He just seemed phony, like he was hiding something," she replied.

Then came October. Tim and Ashley double-dated with Sarah on several dates that first weekend. She had agreed to two dates with two different men, Dave and Zachery. The date with Zachery was not a good date. All he wanted was to get into her pants and it was obvious. He tried to kiss her after dinner and invited her back to his place for nightcaps. Sarah wanted to go, but with Ashley's help, resisted the idea.

The date with Dave went much nicer and Ashley was starting to warm up to him more. After the date with Dave, Ashley informed Sarah of her feelings about him that first night. She also confessed she may have been too judgmental and would give him a chance. Sarah told them both that she liked Dave and would love it to work out between them. Ashley agreed. Dave did not ask her for another date that night, but instead, called her the following day and asked. Sarah had thought something had gone wrong, until she received the phone call the next morning around 10 a.m.

They dated throughout the month of October and Sarah had let him know that she was keeping all options open, seeing other guys and such. He was not happy about this news, but accepted it with a grain of salt. He had told her that he liked her and wanted to see where things could go, but made no promises about anything, but agreed to keep his options open, too.

Dave and Sarah ran into each other at the gym that week, and he asked her to join him for a smoothie after their work out, to which she agreed. They talked for a while and enjoyed each other's company. When it was time for her to leave and get Brandon, they said their goodbyes, and she leaned in to kiss him. It was a gentle kiss, a little awkward but sweet and appropriate for their surroundings. This was technically their third date after all and Sarah felt it was right. She had made him wait this long, and he had been a gentleman about it. She called Ashley and informed her of their chance meeting and her actions on her way to pick up Brandon. She also told her that after their date this weekend she was going to give him a little more romantic kiss. She then asked for Ashley to help her stay out of the bedroom with him as she was getting the urge to have sex. Ashley had agreed to this and reminded her of the rules. Sarah was very grateful to have Ashley in her life and helping her in this way.

Sarah had been promiscuous since she was fifteen and had never been in a long-term relationship. She knew it was time to grow up and try to settle down, but the urges still persisted and were growing stronger with every date she had. Around Halloween, Ashley suggested she and Tim take Brandon trick-or-treating and let

Sarah have a nice one-on-one date with Dave. Sarah agreed and asked Ashley to meet her at her house at 5 p.m. Halloween night, her date was at 6:30 p.m.

Tim made it to Sarah's house about 5:15 p.m., and he and Ashley dressed as mummies. Brandon was a ghost, and they went out trick-or-treating at 5:45 p.m. Ashley told Sarah she had her phone and to call her if she needed any help as she walked out the door holding Brandon's little hand. They returned to Sarah's house around 7:30 p.m. and put Brandon to bed, waiting for Sarah to come home.

She returned around 9 p.m. and filled them in on the details of her date. First, she asked how Brandon had come out with the trick-or-treating, and was shown two grocery bags full of candy, and stated they had a wonderful time. Ashley told her he was very well-behaved and easy to get into bed that night with the promise that the candy would be waiting on him in the morning. Then Sarah talked about her date.

It had gone well; they had eaten dinner and then went to a little hole-in-the-wall bar for drinks afterwards. At the bar, she admitted to making out with Dave, kissing him several times. She also thought that it might be time to stop dating others and see where this relationship headed. She admitted that it was Dave that had said no when she asked him to come over to her house. He had refused like a gentleman, knowing the time was not right and remembering the three rules.

Ashley reminded her that she needed to stick to the rules, no matter how hard it might be. She told her masturbation is acceptable, and she needed to remember why she set the rules up in the first place. Over the next week, Ashley and Tim discussed the sexual aspect of Sarah. They decided Sarah might have an addiction to sex. They decided to confront her about it. Friday, while Tim was at work, Ashley went over to Sarah's house to discuss the situation. She had done some research and found an in-house sex addiction service.

Sarah welcomed Ashley into her home with a hug. Once in the den, Ashley started explaining her feelings and the help she can get. Ashley had informed Sarah that there was a trigger that causes sexual addiction and that it could be anything from trauma to drug addiction. After sometime, Ashley finished and asked Sarah what she thought and if she would be willing to give it a try.

"You would have to fly there; it is in California, and it lasts for 45 days," Ashley said in a matter-of-fact tone.

"What about Brandon, would he go with me?" Sarah asked trying to absorb everything that was said that day.

"No, he could stay with Tim and I, while you were away. You know we are good to him, and he loves us," Ashley stated.

"You would do that for me?" Sarah replied as she hugged Ashley.

"Of course, that's what sisters are for." Ashley said.

"Is Tim onboard with this?" Sarah asked

"It was actually his idea," Ashley said.

During the conversation, Ashley had given her a phone number to the facility and Sarah now called the number. She asked a lot of questions, and apparently, she liked the answers she got and asked how soon she could get in.

"I can get in a week from Monday. Is that too soon?" she asked Ashley.

"Book your flight," Ashley replied.

That weekend, Sarah canceled her date with Dave and explained she would be going away for some much-needed help for a month and a half. She asked him to wait on her, but would understand if he saw other people in her absence.

He agreed to wait for her to return. This made Sarah happy; she was beginning to really like Dave.

That night Ashley told Tim about the day's events over dinner. He was ecstatic to hear that Sarah would seek help. After they ate, they decided to go over to Sarah's house and congratulate her in person. Sarah was nervous about leaving Brandon and being gone for that length of time, but Tim helped to ease her fears. He told her that her house was on his way to work and that he could check in on it daily. Ashley could get Brandon to and from daycare and his appointments for tutoring. Tim would stay with Ashley and Brandon on the weekends and that everything would work out fine. They stayed for a couple of hours and then went back to Tim's apartment for the night.

When they awoke Tim wanted to see his little buddy, so they went back to Sarah's. Brandon met them in the driveway, giving them both big hugs. They spent the day at the zoo and went out for ice cream afterwards. Then, Tim asked Brandon if he would like to spend some time at Aunt Ashley's house, letting him know that he would also be there on the weekends. Brandon liked the idea and wanted to go that night. He was a little disappointed when he found out that it would not be for another week.

On the following Friday, Tim took them all out to dinner, including Dave. Sarah had asked him out on Tuesday, as per Tim's request. Brandon stayed with his great-aunt Martha, as he usually did when the adults go out. Sarah had told Dave why she was leaving and where she was going, informing him that they may have to just be friends for a while when she returned. He was not happy about the down grade to friend zone, but knew she was trying to better herself and agreed to this. They talked over dinner. When it came time to leave, Dave wished her the best of luck and told her he would be here for her when she got ready to date again. Before he left, he gave her a kiss on the cheek and that upset Sarah a little bit, but she also understood.

The following Sunday, Tim took Brandon to Ashley's house while Ashley took Sarah to the airport. Sarah did not want Brandon to see her get on a plane and leave. He might not understand, she thought, and had asked for it to happen this way. When Ashley returned home, she was attacked with hugs and kisses from both of the men in her life. Sarah called that night to let Ashley know she had arrived at the hotel and would be at the facility first thing the next morning. Sarah also asked her if it was okay to touch base with her occasionally to which Ashley told her that she had better keep in touch. The time passed quickly for Tim and them, but seemed to drag on for Sarah.

Sarah had group therapy in the mornings, counselor sessions in the afternoon, and was put on antidepressants. There was a little free time during the day, which she would spend thinking about Brandon. She and her counselor came to the understanding that the reason for her sexual appetite was the sudden loss of her parents years ago. She was trying to fill a void left by their absence. This loss had enhanced her depression and this was the only outlet she knew. Sarah had never told Ashley how her parents died, neither had Mark. That was the only taboo subject amongst them.

She called every night around 6 p.m. and filled Ashley in on how things went that day, never talking about anyone in particular except herself and her counselor. The last night, she told Ashley that she needed to talk to her alone when she got back. She asked if Tim would mind, saying it was very important to her and needed to tell her.

She came home a week before Christmas. Ashley, Tim, and Brandon went to pick her up when her noon flight got in. Brandon ran to her jumping into her arms as she debarked the plane and squealed that his mommy was home. They all hugged before getting her luggage off the carousel and leaving the airport. They all went to lunch and talked about how Brandon had missed his mother. When they got to Sarah's house, the men went to play to give the ladies a chance to talk privately. Sarah started talking about what happened to Mark and her parents.

"When we were kids, we lived in an average-sized three-bedroom, two-story house on an average street. Mostly white-collar workers lived near us and had no Idea that Dad had inherited his father's business and money. The only thing we had that was different from all the neighbors was we had Uncle Henry, my dad's brother. He was the principal at our school and would take us daily to and from school. We were in the start of the sixth grade when it happened. Uncle Henry dropped us off after school that day. Mark had to go to football practice and I had studying to do. Mark always got a ride from his football coach to practice and went down the street to his house. He only lived a few houses down.

I heard something but did not know what it was at the time, so I entered the house. As I entered, paying absolutely no attention to anything, I dropped my book bag. When I went to retrieve it, I noticed it was wet. I started to pay more attention at that point and saw it had fallen into a pool of blood. I saw my mother laying on the floor just a few feet from where I stood. She had been shot to death, then I saw my father in the entry way to the kitchen. He also was surrounded in a pool of blood, but he reached out towards me and tried to speak but no words came out. That's when he grabbed me. He must have been hiding behind the door as I came in. He put a gloved hand over my mouth to keep me quiet. He slid the other into my panties and fondled me. I bit the one hand as I fought back, and he released me enough that I was able to get away. I ran to the neighbor's house, and they called the police. By the time the ambulance arrived, my dad was dead as well. Mark had no idea any of this had happened until Uncle Henry picked him up at football practice that evening. We bounced around the aunts' and uncles' houses for a few months and then finally settled with Aunt Martha. They found out it was a young man who had been battling with drug addiction that had done it. He confessed when he was caught later that night, trying to sell my mother's jewelry. He said he didn't know anyone was home at the time."

They both were in tears as Sarah finished telling the details of that fateful day.

Sarah knew Ashley would tell Tim everything she had learned that afternoon and was okay with it, but did not want Brandon to hear. The two friends held each other. Ashley was in complete disbelief. She often wondered why Mark had never told her about the circumstance of their parents' death, but now understood.

After a while, Tim came out with Brandon, saying that the boys were starting to get hungry. He thought it might be a good idea for them to go to dinner since it was almost Brandon's bedtime. So, they went and ate. During their evening meal Tim asked Sarah if she would be able to see Dave before Christmas, or did she need to wait until after the new year began. She informed him they would have to wait until after Ashley's wedding to start dating, but she could see him as a friend.

"I do like him and would like to have him as a friend," Sarah sheepishly said.

"We can help with that, if you want to build a friendship with Dave," Ashley said quickly.

"Yeah, we can all go out as friends, but only as friends. That means no kissing while we are out and that includes us," Tim agreed.

"Why don't you call him and see if we can get together tomorrow afternoon so the two of you can talk about everything. I do mean everything, including your parents' death and the rehab," Ashley stated, giving Tim a heads up to their future conversation that night.

Sarah called Dave, and he agreed to see her as a friend the following day. He was glad that she had gotten home safe and sound. They agreed to meet up in town, and then drive to Ashley's house for a little privacy knowing the sensitivity of the discussion they were to have.

That night when they got back to Ashley's house, she told Tim everything that Sarah had said earlier that day, forgetting and omitting nothing. Again, she cried for her dear friend and sister as she told the story. Tim held her tight on the couch. When she was through recounting the conversation, Tim kissed her and suggested they go to bed for the night. They hugged and kissed one more time as they went to their separate bedrooms.

Before saying goodnight, Ashley said, "You could come into my room and keep me company tonight. That would be okay with me."

"I would love to, but remember the third rule," Tim said begrudgingly.

She loved him even more for that. Instead of Tim, she curled up with her favorite blanket and quickly went to sleep. Tim thought to himself that this not kissing thing is going to be hard to perform, as he too drifted off to sleep.

The next morning, she awoke at her usual time and climbed into her large soaker tub for a bath. She did not know Tim was already up and planning to surprise her with breakfast in bed. He had only been up for a few minutes and had not had time to prepare everything yet. When he was done cooking, he brought a tray of biscuits and gravy, two scrambled eggs, and two sausage patties along with a glass of orange juice and a cup of coffee to her room. As he entered her room, she was exiting the bathroom still dripping wet. She quickly jumped back in bed hoping that he had seen nothing, but he had seen enough. He placed the tray on her bed and quickly stepped out of her room, without saying a word. After she got dressed, she found him in the kitchen cleaning up, and they apologized to each other as she blushed.

"How much did you see?" she asked.

"Enough to not need an imagination anymore at night," he replied. "Again, I am sorry for catching you coming out of the tub, but I thought. . .," he started saying when she interrupted him with a kiss.

"That's all you get for now; you are being a bad boy," she said coyly, and blushed again.

They were to meet Dave and Sarah at Rusty's that afternoon at 2 p.m. and it was just now 6:45 p.m. They both tried to put what had happened behind them, but both wanted to break the third rule that morning. Around nine, Ashley called Sarah and told her what had happened. She also informed her she had to take care of business before getting dressed, a fact that she did not tell Tim.

They left the house at 1 p.m. and made it to Rusty's at 2 p.m. on the dot. Sarah was already inside talking with Dave. They ordered a late lunch and ate, then headed back to Ashley's house. Once there Sarah, told Dave everything over a glass of wine. Dave was saddened by what happened to her parents and watched as Ashley comforted her. Then Sarah told him why she had left so abruptly and explained that she was getting help for a sexual addiction. She told him that she could not date for a while, but that Tim and Ashley had come up with a possible solution.

"I do like you and want to date you, but can we just be friends for a while first?" Sarah asked.

"I like you, too. I am okay with being friends," Dave responded, then he started to tell his story.

"I fell in love with Susan in high school, our junior year. We dated and finally married in our sophomore year in college. We both waited until we were married to have sex, although it was hard. We both got our bachelor's degrees and I went on to law school. One day in January, about four years ago, someone was traveling too fast for the road conditions, hit some black ice, and crossed the center line, hitting my wife head-on, and they both died. We had found out the day before that she was three months pregnant with our first child. I have had a hard time dating anyone since. In fact, I hadn't asked anyone out until I asked you. I miss my wife dearly and felt like if I were to go out with someone else, I would be cheating on her. So, it has been four years next month since I lost my wife. I am willing to build a friendship with you before we start dating. . .to give you the time you need to get help," he said with a tear in his eye.

His story sounded familiar to Ashley. She explained about Mark and what happened to him over coffee. Little did she know at the time, but it was Mark that had taken her life that January day. After talking a while, they figured it out and Dave told Ashley that he had no ill feelings for Mark. It was an accident and the only thing he blamed this tragedy on was the weather. He did admit that now, more than ever, he wanted to meet Brandon. The hour was starting to get late, Sarah and Dave decided to go to their own houses for the night. As they left, Tim and Ashley talked about how much of a small world it turned out to be.

About 9 a.m. Christmas morning, Sarah went over to Ashley's with Brandon. Ashley had gotten him some gifts and really wanted to see him. Tim arrived 30 minutes later with his arms full of presents for all three of them. They drank coffee as Brandon opened each gift with awe. Ashley had gotten a package of bath bombs, bath oils, and bubble bath solution. Sarah got a bottle of perfume and a coupon that Tim had made that said he would bail her out of any jam she might get into. It was obvious that their friendship had grown since the night of the incident. They had been spending a lot of time with each other over the last few months and had gotten very close. Tim was already thinking of her as his sister. Ashley was delighted by this fact. Around noon, Sarah and Brandon left to see the rest of her family, starting with Aunt Martha. Tim and Ashley spent the day lounging around the house watching movies.

Tim suggested they have a New Year's Eve party at Ashley's house and invite Sarah, Brandon, and Dave. So, they planned it and made the phone calls. Tim spent the week at his apartment packing for the move in a month to Ashley's. He was taking his time putting things in boxes and decided to start taking them to Ashley's home. He could leave them in the garage or in the storage room until he moved in officially.

New Year's Eve went as planned, Brandon was out for the count by 10 p.m. and the adults sat around talking, and drinking wine, beer, and coffee. At the stroke of midnight, Sarah pulled Dave to her and gave him a kiss before remembering their arrangement. As she was apologizing, he told her it was a good luck kiss for the new year. A tradition observed by many, and to prove his point, he kissed Ashley on the cheek. Everyone was fine with the turn of events that night. Ashley had set up two more extra bedrooms for her guests to stay the night, knowing they were going to be drinking, and informed them that they could not leave.

"Consider yourselves kidnapped for the night," she told all of them.

With four of her extra bedrooms occupied, she kissed Tim goodnight and curled up with her favorite blanket and drifted off to sleep. She awoke a short time later to Sarah's voice.

"Are you awake?" Sarah asked tentatively.

"I am now," Ashley responded. "What's up?"

"I am having a hard time not going into Dave's room and having sex with him. I need your help," Sarah explained.

At this point, Ashley pulled the covers on the other side of the bed down and told her to sleep with her. Ashley was usually a light sleeper and would be glad to help Sarah stay accountable. Ashley knew the power of sexual urges mixed with alcohol could cause Sarah to regress, but wanted her to know that she was happy to help. The next morning, they all slept in until 8 a.m., when Brandon woke the ladies up by jumping onto the bed.

That morning Dave and Tim made breakfast for everyone. Brandon ate two pancakes and a sausage patty. Brandon belched as he finished his breakfast, then turned red in embarrassment.

"That shattered windows there, little buddy," Dave said, quickly embarrassing him even more as they all laughed. "You have a wonderful son, Sarah," he continued.

She thought it may have been sarcastically stated, but Dave thought Brandon was a wonderful child. He could not wait to get to know him better. After they finished breakfast and cleaned up their mess, they went their separate ways; each going to their own homes, including Tim. That afternoon, Sarah called Ashley and thanked her again for keeping her accountable the previous night. She invited her and Tim over to her house for Brandon's birthday. It was coming up in only 10 days. Ashley suggested that they also invite Dave. Sarah was overjoyed at the thought.

January 11th was a hard day for all of them. Each had lost someone that they had loved. Even Tim was saddened by the loss of his good friend, but no one showed it around Brandon. This was his special day as he would only turn four once. For his birthday, he got some new first grade reading level books and some new toys. Brandon's favorite was the books. He knew that he was going to start preschool in the fall and looked forward to it. He called it 'all day school.' Again, Dave told Sarah that she had a wonderful child, this time he added that he is glad that he is getting to know him. After the party, they all went to Rusty's for lunch.

The four of them saw each other almost every weekend thereafter. Always as a foursome on Friday nights when Dave was there. Tim and Ashley reserved Saturdays for themselves and Ashley usually went to Sarah's on Sundays. The winter that year was pretty mild with very little snow or ice. The average temperature was in the twenties and rarely did it feel below zero. Tim finished moving in on the 24th and settled in nicely. As spring started to immerge, they all had gotten busy with the plans for Tim and Ashley's wedding.

Sarah paid for Tim's parents to fly in for this joyous event and asked them to stay with her and Brandon. They were thrilled to stay with her and told her so many times before their flight. They were to fly in a week before the wedding, and would stay for a week afterwards, giving his parents a two-week vacation near him. Although they had never met in person, Ashley and Tim's parents had talked over Zoom and on the phone regularly. Tim's mother was looking forward to meeting her soon-to-be daughter-in-law. Their flight landed at 2 p.m. May 5th. Tim and Ashley met them at the airport. Ashley had brought flowers for Tim's mother and a new Stetson cowboy hat for his father. She knew this would make them feel good after their 3-hour flight. Introductions were made, and they all hugged then they left for Sarah's house. On the 15-minute drive, they talked about Brandon and the wedding.

"He is going to be the ring bearer," Tim said happily. "Just wait till you meet him."

Ashley informed them that Sarah was to be her maid-of-honor and Tim asked his dad to be his best man. Brandon met them in the drive way as they pulled in with Sarah standing in the doorway. He gave them all hugs, yelling that Uncle Tim had come to see him. Molly, Tim's mother, asked if there was anything she could do for the wedding, and after some consideration, Ashley asked if she would honor her by giving her away. She was overjoyed at the thought of this.

That night Ashley cooked dinner for them at Sarah's house, and they all sat around talking until 10 p.m. Tim stated that he had work in the morning, and he and Ashley headed home. Dave called Sarah around 10:30 p.m., and they talked for about an hour. Just before they hung up Sarah told Dave that she was glad he was in her life and that she loved him, quickly adding that she loved him as a friend. She thought it was more than that, but could not let it go there yet. They had seen a lot of each other over the past few months, always with Tim and Ashley present, but in the last few weeks, they started talking almost nightly on the phone.

Sarah took Tim's parents to Ashley's house the next day to plan the layout for the wedding and do some finishing touches by the pond. Sarah and Frank, Tim's Father, built a wedding arch and set up the seating arrangements. It was going to be a small wedding with just a few guests, but it was going to be beautiful, Sarah thought. While they were outside, Ashley showed her wedding dress to Molly. Molly loved the cut and thought her son was one lucky man. She knew that he would be stunned by her beauty in that dress. Around 1 p.m., Sarah had to leave to get Brandon, and brought him back to Ashley's home.

For dinner that night, the four of them met up with Tim at Rusty's. The adults ordered soup and salads, while Brandon had a kid's meal of chicken nuggets and mac-and-cheese. They talked about the upcoming wedding and their friend Dave. Sarah asked Ashley to join her in the bathroom for a second and informed her about her phone calls with Dave. She even confessed to making a slip the night before by telling him she loved him, explaining that she had tried to cover it up. Sarah admitted that she was falling for Dave and could not wait to start dating him again. They all kept pretty busy that week and then came Saturday, May 12th, the day of the wedding.

Tim and his dad dressed early and headed out to the pond that morning. The wedding was set for noon. Molly helped Ashley get into her dress, while Sarah and Brandon waited on the other guests and the minister. They all arrived by 11:15 a.m. except Dave. The wedding was beautiful. Tim actually gasped when Ashley stepped out of the woods in her wedding gown. She had never looked so beautiful to him before. After the wedding was completed, they all returned to the house for the reception. That is when Sarah checked her phone, seeing that Dave had called her at 10:45 a.m. explaining that he would be there around 11:30 a.m. After the reception, she called Dave to find out why he had not shown, and a female answered his phone.

"Hello, David Palmer's phone," the mysterious women said.

"This is Sarah. Is Dave there?" she said getting a little worried but thinking he may be at the office.

"This is Nurse Brown. How do you know David?" she asked.

"I am his girlfriend!" Sarah spat out. "Why is a Nurse Brown answering his phone?"

"Dear, I am sorry to inform you that David was involved in an auto accident this morning and is in the hospital. They are running tests on him, but he is in critical condition," Nurse Brown stated matter-of-factly.

"Can I come see him?" Sarah said through her tears.

"Yes, you may. He is in ICU 1310. Just don't upset him and understand he is slipping in and out of consciousness. He does have several broken bones and a collapsed lung. Like I said, he is in critical condition," Nurse Brown stated flatly.

Sarah informed Ashley of the situation and was told to go see him. Ashley and Tim would go shortly, but they had to change first. Molly told Sarah to go and leave Brandon with her and Frank at Sarah's house; they would be fine. Once she got to the hospital, she quickly found the elevators and went up to his room. He was sleeping as she entered, so she went to the nurse's station to get more information on his condition and what happened.

"He was heading east on Route 19 when a semi coming down the hill lost control and jackknifed. The trailer crossed into oncoming traffic and hit him. He was airlifted to the hospital with a broken leg, three broken ribs, several broken vertebrae, a collapsed lung on his left side, and numerous bruises and contusions. We have him medicated to help with the pain, but are not sure if there are any brain injuries yet. The CT scan is scheduled for tomorrow morning. He may never walk again," his nurse said.

A few minutes later, Ashley and Tim showed up, and Sarah filled them in on what she had learned. They waited in the waiting room while Sarah waited in Dave's room for him to wake up enough to talk. He woke after an hour of her sitting there, although he was not too coherent. He thanked her for coming and apologized for not making it to the wedding. She told him about Ashley and Tim being there as well, as he drifted back to sleep.

"Visiting hours are over, I am sorry, but you are going to have to leave." The nurse said as she entered his room. "You can come back tomorrow at nine. His CT is scheduled for 10 a.m. and it should not take more than a half an hour," she continued.

Sarah gave him a gentle kiss and left the room, going back to her waiting friends.

The next morning, the CT scan came back normal and he was more alert in the afternoon. He would have to stay in the hospital for a week or so and needed physical therapy after his release. He would also need to have someone to take care of him for a while. Sarah volunteered for that duty. He would be out of commission for at least six weeks.

During the 10 days Dave spent in the hospital, Sarah and Ashley discussed the need he had for his friends. They agreed that he could stay at Sarah's, and she could get him to physical therapy and back. She had a bedroom on the main floor and it would be good for Dave to use, since climbing the stairs might be hard at first. They proposed this idea to Dave, and he thanked them for their kindness. He agreed to stay at Sarah's, but only until he got back on his feet.

Over the next six weeks, Ashley and Tim came over several times during the week and spent most of the weekends at Sarah's. Ashley could see Sarah was getting closer to Dave. They made a cute couple. Dave had physical therapy three days a week and started using crutches after the first week at Sarah's. Sarah continued to call Ashley nightly and kept her informed of her feelings. Sarah knew she had broken the second rule, but under the circumstances it was inevitable. She was growing fonder of Dave by the day. Watching him fight to get back in good health showed he was a determined man. She knew she loved him by the end of the six weeks. Once he was better, they started dating again. This time she kept to the rules. All three of them.

Tim hated the fact that he had to be away from his bride so much each day, and they decided that he did not need to work. So, he resigned while Dave was on the mend at Sarah's. Tim and Ashley finally consummated their wedding after Dave moved back to his house. They had waited and spent their time with Sarah and Dave. They had stayed in separate rooms during this time. The day Dave left Sarah's house, Ashley and Tim finally moved into the same room. After Sarah called Ashley that night, they went to bed together for the first time since they were married. They made love together for the first time. That first night was glorious for both of them. Tim remembered seeing her coming out of the bathroom months ago as he undressed her for the first time. He had kissed her naked body many times in his mind, now he was doing it for real. He kissed her stomach and worked his way slowly to her mouth as she lay naked on the bed, his engorged manhood waiting patiently for what was to come. They made love twice that night and once the next morning.

Sarah called around 9 a.m. asking them to come over. She had gotten used to someone else at her house and was feeling lonely. She knew she could call Dave and talk with him, but she also knew he was trying to get back to work at his law firm. She wanted physical company, but called him while she waited for Ashley and Tim to arrive. They spent the day together. Around 1 p.m., Sarah said she needed to go pickup Brandon, but Tim volunteered this chore. Brandon was glad that Uncle Tim had picked him up from daycare and even more happy when they went for ice cream before returning home.

Tim knew the ladies needed to talk privately and tried to give them some time to do it. It had been a while since their wedding, the last time they could talk openly with each other without someone else being within earshot. Tim's parents had left just a few days before Dave came to stay at Sarah's house. Those few days were spent at the hospital with Dave.

When Tim and Brandon got back, they went to Brandon's room and played, letting the women talk freely. Sarah admitted her feelings for Dave and told her that she was going to date him starting that weekend. She also informed her that she was going to abide by the three rules for that day forward. Her rehabilitation was going well, and she did not want to ruin that. Her counselor had already given her the okay to date and even given her kudos for helping Dave in his time of need. She asked if they would join her and Dave for dinner on Friday night, to which Ashley politely declined. Ashley felt that Sarah could do this one date alone. Dave was not one hundred percent back to normal, but was getting there. Ashley knew that Sarah and Dave had some things to talk about and that it would be best if they were alone to do that. Ashley told her that she was just a phone call away and could talk to her if she needed any help.

# Chapter 3

Dave, being a family law attorney, hired a legal team to go after the trucking company and the driver that hit him. He knew the truck driver had been speeding, causing the accident. They had already admitted fault and offered one hundred thousand dollars in compensation. Dave felt like this offer was missing a zero or two and wanted to make then correct the error. He damn near died, had medical bills totaling the offered amount, not to even mention the pain and suffering that he was still enduring. He wanted what was rightfully his. Dave had started calling his office the last week he stayed at Sarah's house, making plans for his return.

Once back, his first few cases were going to be simple divorce cases. He knew they would not require too much work. He was sitting at his desk that first day, going over one of the files, when Sarah called him on his cell phone. He answered on the second ring.

"Hello, beautiful," He started the conversation, "How are you doing in that empty house, all alone?"

"I'm managing," she said with a chuckle. "Since we are going to date again, now that you are mostly healed up, I have to remind you of the three rules. Starting now we have to keep to the rules for both of our sake's. You cannot come over to my house and I cannot go to yours anymore. We must meet in a public place, no kissing for the first couple of dates, and no sex until. . ." She left the last words fall off, knowing that she wanted him to ask her for her hand in marriage already.

She knew she had fallen in love with him over the last six weeks and that he had stayed with her. She had restrained herself from doing anything to jeopardize her therapy and rehabilitation. Even though she wanted to at least kiss him, she hadn't. After they both agreed to restarting the ground rules, she told him that she had Ashley coming over and had to go, adding that she knew he was a busy man and his time was valuable. After she hung up the phone she whispered, "I love you."

Dave knew she had called to hear his voice and that she needed to hear the rules again, for her sake. He was alright with it and let her repeat them whenever she needed to. As he hung up the phone, he too whispered the same three little words that he had not said since his wife had died. He looked at the photo of his late wife that he had placed on his desk and removed it, placing it in one of his drawers. This was going to be a new chapter in his life, and he needed to move on, even though he still loved her. Over the last week, he had ordered a new car, since his had been totaled, and had it delivered to his house. His auto insurance covered that much.

Even though he still used crutches to get around, he still would go to court. His first case was scheduled for that afternoon. It was an amicable divorce, shared custody of the children, and both parties had agreed on how to split the assets they had. The case only took about 20 minutes, but gave a boost of confidence to himself. He now knew that he was going to be okay. Granted, he had tried cases before the accident, his nerves and self-esteem had been destroyed by the near-death experience. He had also began questioning his worth as a man. The phone call from Sarah boosted his confidence in that aspect, but he was still nervous, thinking that she might reject him after all they had been through.

They went out that Friday night, as they had previously done, this time not as friends but as potential partners. They talked and even had a few laughs over dinner. Saturday, they met up with Ashley and Tim at their house and had a cook out. Tim cooked hamburgers and hot dogs on the grill and the ladies made side dishes in the kitchen, while Brandon told Dave about his tutor. She was a sophomore in college, studying elementary education, with the hopes and dreams of becoming an elementary teacher.

"Her name is Miss Hannah. She is old, but not as old as you," Brandon said making Dave laugh.

He knew Miss Hannah and knew she was only 19 years old. He had met her on several occasions over the last few months. Dave thought she was a cute young lady, and he knew she would be a great teacher someday. She had been tutoring Brandon for the last two years, and he was very fond of his tutor. He always met her in the driveway with his flashcards in hand and was always wanting to learn more from her. She had a great disposition and Dave could tell she loved spreading knowledge to others. He also knew that she had only a couple of other children she tutored, but to hear her tell it, Brandon was her favorite. She had told Dave several times this fact and was impressed at how well he learned. She even stated that he would probably become valedictorian. Brandon saw Miss Hannah every

Monday, Wednesday, and Friday for about an hour.

Brandon also told Dave about the books he had been trying to read and showed him the one he brought with him. They sat on the couch and read it together, Dave letting Brandon do most of the reading and helping out when needed. Not only had he been practicing his reading and math, but Miss Hannah had him practice his spelling and printing also, which he gladly showed to his friend Dave.

Brandon ate a hot dog and some fries along with a soda, while the adults ate burgers and fries and drank beer. After lunch, they all walked around the woods and finally stopped at the pond. This gave Tim an idea. As it was starting to be summer, they needed to invite Sarah, Brandon, and Dave over for a night of camping by a fire. He suggested this to Ashley, and they agreed it would be best to do it over the Fourth of July weekend. That would give Dave a little more time to heal. It would also give them a few weeks to get some fireworks. Brandon was excited about this new adventure and could not stop talking about it for weeks.

Ashley and Tim bought a new tent that slept six and got air mattresses for them to sleep on. They also got a fire grate to cook on and new sleeping bags for everyone. As the Fourth of July weekend approached, Sarah and Dave talked to each other daily and still kept their date nights. Sarah was a little concerned about the sleeping arrangements and voiced this to Ashley.

"Not to worry, Tim and I will be there and will sleep in between the two of you. Brandon will sleep next to you and I will be on the other side. Nothing will happen, I promise," Ashley stated with certainty, hoping that she was correct.

That weekend, they gathered at Ashley and Tim's house and were told that the tent and campsite had already been set up, surprising them. Ashley had told all three to bring swimsuits, and they could change in the house. After a light lunch, they walked to the pond and went swimming for a while. Dave watched Brandon while the others swam out to the diving platform. Brandon was a good little swimmer, but not good enough to cover the distance to the platform. Dave, still in recovery, had lost his crutches a few days earlier and did not want to chance anything, so he stayed in the shallow waters near the shore. They stayed in the water frolicking for a couple of hours then went inside to take showers and clean up. Ashley's pale skin had reddened to a burnt umber tone, and she was feeling the sunburn already. After her shower, she coated her entire body with aloe lotion and dressed in loose clothing. She had so much fun in the pond, that she had lost track of the time. Brandon also was a little sun burned and Sarah rubbed the lotion on him as well.

After cleaning up, they gathered the cooler and supplies for dinner and headed back to the pond. Tim lit the fire and started cooking the hot dogs and chili that was to be their supper. Dave and Sarah sat at one end of the log and talked while Ashley and Brandon played and read his book again. He was getting better at sounding out the words. He was refusing help on the hard ones, saying he could do it. He reminded her of her late husband, stubborn as all get out. Brandon was determined to read the book on his own.

After dinner, they made s'mores and Brandon ate three. The adults were astonished by how much he put away. As the sun went down, Tim and Dave walked back to the house and got the fireworks. Tim had them all lined up and would be lighting them over the pond. He had gotten some sparklers for Brandon to play with and handed him one. Brandon ran around waving the sparkler as it burned. He felt all grown up, like a little man. After a few sparklers, they lit off the aerial show and Brandon oohed and awed with each one. The show lasted for about an hour, and then they retired to the tent for the night. Once Brandon was asleep, the adults quietly stepped out of the tent and resumed their position on the log, talking late into the night. They made several pots of coffee and drank them as they talked. At one point, Sarah pulled Ashley aside and said she was starting to struggle with her issue.

"I want to have sex with him," Sarah said.

"Then you are human, but not ready to do that yet," Ashley interjected.

"I know, but the urge is getting stronger every time I see him," Sarah said ashamedly.

"I thought that might happen, but you are strong. Strong enough to wait for marriage. I know he feels the same way; I can tell by the way he looks at you. He is still dealing with feelings for you along with the struggle of loving his late wife. Trust me, I understand where he is coming from. I have been there and you helped me through it. I am now here to help you through this time in your life." Ashley's pep talk helped Sarah regain her composure.

The girls hugged and rejoined the guys at the fire. It was almost 1 a.m. when they all went to bed. Brandon was snoring as they entered the tent the second time, causing Ashley to giggle. Ashley awoke the next morning to Brandon stepping on her as he tried to leave the tent. Tim had already gone to the cooler and started breakfast; pancakes and sausage were making the morning air smell good. Sarah and Ashley left the tent together looking for Dave. Tim advised that nature called him back to the house, and he should return shortly. As Tim finished saying this, Dave exited the woods asking where the angels had come from. The ladies knew he was talking about them and both blushed. Brandon went to the edge of the pond and was watching some minnows swim by.

After breakfast, Tim had promised Brandon that he would teach him to fish, but when it came time, it was Dave that taught him. He happily was taking on a father figure roll. Tim and Sarah watched Dave, Brandon, and Ashley fish for a while, before Brandon caught his first fish. It was maybe five inches long and too small to keep, so Dave convinced him to throw it back. Dave explained that you didn't have to keep every fish that you caught. Ashley also caught a fish shortly after Brandon had landed his fish, although Brandon's fish was bigger. After a while they all headed to the house. Ashley offered each of them a bedroom to nap in and said they would go out for dinner that night. Tim went back to the campsite and put everything away, before taking a nap himself. Ashley had waited and kissed him when he returned. She was still feeling the sunburn.

They all slept for a few hours, before Brandon awoke. Sarah was the second one up and slowly crept to the room Dave was sleeping in. She stood in the doorway watching him silently, when to her surprise, he said for her to come in. She did and they kissed. She told Dave at that point she wanted him more than ever and quickly walked out of his room embarrassed at her actions.

They all cleaned up and changed clothes, getting ready to go to town for dinner. Sarah and Dave each drove their own cars while Brandon rode in the truck with Ashley and Tim. They all knew they would be going their separate ways after dinner, but Brandon wanted to go home with Dave that night. The two of them were getting very close and Sarah was ecstatic about that fact.

Over the next few weeks, Dave's law firm picked up a lot of new clients, and he felt swamped by the workload. Although he wanted to see Sarah every Friday night, it was getting to the point that he could not, so they changed date night to Saturdays and made it an all-day event. Tim and Ashley usually met up with them for dinner. During their day dates, Dave usually took Sarah and Brandon to a movie, show, or a museum. Although he wanted to spend time alone with Sarah, Brandon was part of the package deal.

About a month after the camping trip, Ashley and Tim took Brandon home with them on a Friday night to give Sarah a little more freedom for Saturday. They said they would return him at dinner, if she was good. If not, then they would be forced to keep him forever. Sarah laughed, thanking them for the opportunity to see Dave alone for a change.

"Brandon is a great child, Sarah. I can't wait the seven to eight months to get my own," Ashley announced over dinner that night.

She and Tim had kept this secret for almost a week and it took a while for Sarah to realize what Ashley had said.

"Do. . .do you. . .do you mean that. . .," Sarah stammered.

"Yes, we are pregnant," Ashley said radiantly as she held Tim's hand.

They had a reason to celebrate that night. Everyone was drinking except Ashley and Brandon. He had a soda, and she drank iced tea with lemon. After dinner, the ladies went to the restroom to talk about the pregnancy in private, while the men stayed at the table and ordered drinks.

"Tim, I need to talk to you about something important. Can we meet up tomorrow for a little friendly chat?" Dave inquired.

"Sure, I can get away for a couple of hours. I'll let Ash know that we are meeting up for drinks," Tim stated cheerfully.

"I would rather you not tell her that I will be there. I don't want her thinking anything bad," Dave said shyly.

"Where do you want to meet?" Tim asked.

Dave wrote his office address on a napkin and handed it to him. Tim agreed not to tell Ashley and said he would be there. The ladies returned after another five minutes, then they stayed for another hour until Brandon started falling asleep at the table.

The next day, Tim told Ashley that he needed to do some running around town and that he would be back in a few hours. He left just before noon making sure he had the address Dave had given him. He arrived and waited for Dave to arrive. Dave arrived a few minutes later and let him into his office. After some small talk, Tim could see that Dave was getting very nervous. Tim asked what was making him nervous and Dave reached into his top drawer and pulled out a piece of paper, handing it to Tim.

"Read this, please," Dave said nervously.

"Dear David Palmer," the letter started out.

"We are making a settlement offer unto you for the accident that occurred earlier this year. We have determined that our driver was the sole cause of said accident. We apologize for the delay and would like to settle out of court for the sum of $10 million. Once you accept this offer, you will receive the money via a certified check in approximately five business days." The letter continued, but Tim stopped reading.

"Are you going to settle?" Tim Asked Dave.

"I received this letter on Monday. Friday, I got this." Dave said handing him the certified check.

"Congratulations," Tim nearly shouted. "Why all the secrecy?"

"Yesterday, I bought this and wanted your blessings," Dave said, as he pulled an engagement ring out of the same drawer. "I want to ask Sarah to marry me and I want to adopt Brandon as my own. I trust our friendship and I know that you and Ashley know Sarah best. I was hoping you could help me propose to her."

Dave explained he wanted to do something special and Tim agreed to help. Over the next couple of hours, they came up with a game plan. That week, Tim had a hard time keeping the secret from Sarah and an even harder time keeping it from Ashley. On Saturday, all four of them went out to dinner and Brandon went to Aunt Martha's house, as per Tim's request. During dinner, a dozen red roses were delivered to their table with an envelope. On the envelope was Sarah's name. She opened the envelope and pulled out a small card that read "Thank You" on the front. As she opened the card and read it, Dave stood to his feet.

"Thank you for giving me such good care and so much love over the past year. I love you." The card was signed with Dave's name.

As she finished reading the card, she noticed Dave was standing next to the high-top table they were seated at. He was holding something in his hands. This was getting all too real for Sarah, so she drank her entire beer.

"Sarah, I love you and have for a while. I know you love me, too, and I want you to accept my hand in marriage. Will you marry me?" Dave looked at her and said on one knee.

Ashley was as surprised as Sarah and could tell Tim had something to do with this by the shit-eating grin he had on his face. Sarah could not talk she was so taken aback, until Ashley asked her what her answer was. Sarah was finally able to talk and said yes to his question. He then informed her that he would also like to adopt

Brandon. She and Ashley were overjoyed with this prospect.

That night after leaving the restaurant, Dave and Sarah went to pick up Brandon. Sarah told Aunt Martha the good news, as Dave asked Brandon if he could marry his mother and adopt him. Brandon, being a typical four-year-old, did not quite understand the importance of the question, but still said he would love it. Aunt Martha was happy to see Sarah finally settling down and could tell Dave would make a great father to Brandon. After everyone hugged Dave, Brandon and Sarah left Aunt Martha's. Dave dropped off Sarah and Brandon at her car that was still in the restaurant's parking lot, and they went to their perspective homes. The following day, Brandon started preschool and all he could talk about was the fact that he was getting a new daddy.

That afternoon, Miss Hannah stopped by Sarah's house.

"I am sorry, did I forget to tell you that Brandon's preschool started today, he won't be home for another 30 minutes," Sarah stated ashamed.

"No ma'am, you told me last week. I actually came to see you. I need some advice and don't feel comfortable going to my parents for it," Miss Hannah said nervously.

Sarah invited her in, and they talked for a little while. Finally, Miss Hannah got to the point. She explained that she was seeing this guy who was a junior in college with her and had been dating him for almost a year. He was starting to pressure her for sex, and she was scared.

"He is a nice guy, but I don't know if I am ready for that kind of commitment, yet," Miss Hannah elaborated. "I respect you and your opinion. I wanted to ask your advice on sex."

Sarah told her about Ashley's three simple rules and explained how they help you find true love. She explained the difference between sex and love the best she could, and they talked until the school bus dropped Brandon off at the house, and then they started the tutoring session. Brandon told Miss Hannah about Dave asking him if he could be his dad before the session began, and Sarah showed off the ring. As Miss Hannah left, she thanked Sarah again for listening to her and for the advice. She told Brandon that she would see him Wednesday and headed towards her car. Sarah called Ashley that night after talking to Dave and told her about what happened with Miss Hannah.

The next few weeks flew by. As the days started to get shorter, Dave and Sarah saw each other every weekend. The first part of October Dave asked if he could take Brandon trick-or-treating that year and asked Sarah to go along with them. Sarah was delighted and said that it was a date, asking only that Ashley and Tim tag along. Ashley had always been there for Brandon on Halloween, and she did not want that to change.

Dave and Sarah tried to set a date and location for the wedding, but nothing sounded right until Ashley suggested her house. The wedding arch was still up by the pond, and they could use the space for their families. They decided that a spring wedding was a good idea as well. Sarah inquired about April with Dave, and he agreed to April 19th. It was going to be a beautiful wedding. Aunt Martha and Ashley were going to plan it all together. Ashley told Sarah the only thing she needed to worry with was her wedding gown. Between the three ladies, they would find the perfect one.

Aunt Martha met them at the tailor's shop the following Monday, and they picked a dress similar to the one Ashley had. Aunt Martha paid for the dress and Sarah's measurements were taken. They were told the dress would be ready for delivery around the middle of January. They decided to use the same caterer that Ashley had used and the same florist. They ordered seating for 150 people and hired a designer to help spruce up the area by the pond. They had completed all this before Halloween night.

The four adults and Brandon went out that Halloween night. Dave accompanied Brandon to most of the doors, allowing Ashley and Tim the pleasure occasionally. Sarah just wanted to watch her precious child having all the fun. She thought again that Dave would be a great father to Brandon. Brandon raked in three grocery bags of candy that day and insisted that "Daddy Dave" take some.

As Thanksgiving approached, Ashley suggested they all meet at her house for Thanksgiving brunch. She and Tim would fix the turkey and some sides, allowing the others to bring what they wanted. When everyone finally arrived Thanksgiving Day, there was enough food to feed an army for a week. Dave brought a fried turkey, dressing, mashed potatoes, and several casseroles. Sarah smoked a turkey and brought it along with dressing and green bean and cheesy-potato casseroles. Everyone was astonished by the feast set before them, so much so that Tim suggested they send some of the food to the homeless shelter for them to enjoy. Ashley,

Dave, and Sarah all agreed happily. They packed up two turkeys, dressing, and three casseroles and took the hour drive to the homeless shelter. The shelter was overjoyed to receive the bountiful blessing; they also said they were overcrowded and did not know if they had enough food for everyone, but this donation would be enough for sure.

They had learned that the shelter had only 100 beds and was housing almost 200 people, many having to sleep on the floors. This gave Dave an idea. Over the next week, he discussed making a monetary donation to the shelter with Sarah, and she brought it up to Tim and Ashley. They all thought it would be a great idea to help the less fortunate and decided to donate a total of $10 million. Dave and Sarah each would donate $2.5 million and Tim and Ashley would donate the rest. The shelter could add on a wing and add 150 beds. Dave had already done the research and had procured a contractor before they made the donation. Work on the new wing would start in the spring.

That winter was colder than normal, and they got five feet of snow a week before Christmas, making it difficult for Tim and Ashley to leave their home. In town, it was a little better due to the fact that the snowplows were out. Tim finally dug them out a few days before Sarah, Dave, and Brandon were to arrive for their Christmas party. By this time, Ashley was showing a decent baby bump and was often complaining about heartburn to Tim. That day, before everyone arrived, she told Tim that it felt like butterflies in her stomach. She had a doctor's appointment for a sonogram the following week and would find out the sex of the baby then. During the Christmas party, they all took turns feeling the baby bump. When Brandon felt the bump, the baby kicked, scaring him a little bit. Sarah explained to Brandon that he did not do anything wrong, but that the baby was just moving around trying to get comfortable.

During her doctor's visit they found out that the baby was progressing well and doing good. They also found out that Ashley was not having one baby, but two. The twins were both little girls and should be delivered around April 20th. Ashley could not wait to inform Sarah and called her while the doctor was still in the room. Sarah was overjoyed and started planning a baby shower for her. They talked the entire hour that it took Tim to drive to Ashley's home and then an hour afterwards. The baby shower would be in February at Sarah's house. She would invite all of Ashley's friends and then asked Ashley if they had a nursery set up yet. They had not done so, but Tim had been working on it since they got home from the doctor's visit.

That week, Tim and Ashley turned the bedroom Tim had slept in previously into a beautiful nursery with two cribs and rocking chairs for both of them. They knew they were going to be busy over the next few years and started planning for this. Tim was already looking into schools for their daughters, even though that was still six years away. By the end of that week, he had the girls going to Stanford and becoming doctors. Ashley had to bring reality back in and told him to chill out, adding that the girls could choose where they went to college and what they made of themselves.

The New Year's Eve party that year was held at Sarah's house upon Ashley's request. Ashley knew this was breaking the second rule but thought it would be better for everyone involved since the roads had gotten worse with added snowfall. Tim and Ashley could stay the night in one room and Dave could use another. Brandon was out again by 10 p.m. and the adults had drinks downstairs while watching the ball drop in Time Square. Ashley actually allowed herself to have a small glass of champaign at midnight, the first alcohol she'd had since finding out that she was pregnant. The party continued into the early hours of the next morning. The new year arrive with another three feet of snow and temperatures in the negative teens for a high.

Miss Hannah had taken the winter break off from tutoring Brandon as usual and returned to her job the Monday following New Year's Day. She seemed a little frazzled when she arrived at Sarah's house, causing Sarah to pull her aside and ask if she was okay.

"No ma'am, not really." Miss Hannah stated absently, "I told my boyfriend about the three simple rules you shared with me, and he agreed to them. Then, over Christmas he proposed. I told him that I would have to think about it and would give him my answer tonight. He wants to go to the Justice of the Peace on Friday; I really don't know what to do. I know I love him, but what if he is asking just to have sex with me? We are still in college and have nowhere to live as a married couple. I told my parents about this, and they kicked me out of their house. I am now couch surfing until I can find a place of my own."

Hannah sat there on the couch crying.

Sarah, knowing what the poor girl had to be going through, told her that she had a place at her house if she wanted it, under the condition that she remained in school. She also told Hannah, that if Hannah wanted to marry him, then they both could live there rent-free until finishing college. Sarah knew Dave would be okay with this and Hannah thanked her. She was able to get her head together enough to tutor Brandon, and afterwards, call her boyfriend to let him know about the generous offer Sarah had made. After her phone call, Hannah asked Sarah if she would be a witness on Friday, and she agreed.

After Hannah left, she called Dave and informed him of the arrangement she had made. Then she called Ashley and asked her to be a second witness on Friday, explaining the situation to her. Ashley had some hesitations, but agreed for the sake of young love. Hannah's boyfriend had been saving his money for a year and had gotten her a small engagement ring at a pawnshop in town. Hannah showed it to Sarah when she came over on Wednesday. On Friday, Sarah drove to Ashley's house to pick her up for Hannah's wedding.

After the wedding, Hannah and her new husband, Ryan, had the rest of the day off from school. Ryan was an awkward nineteen-year-old kid, and Ashley warmed up to him quickly. They spent the rest of the day setting up a room at Sarah's house for the kids. Ryan had a part-time job as an overnight stocker at one of the supermarkets in town and had to work that night, leaving the girls at home with Brandon. They stayed up late talking and Hannah got to know Ashley well. They all told their stories, making Hannah feel like one of the gang. Hannah had not known a lot about Ashley before that night, but quickly hit it off with her. Their friendship blossomed that night and would continue to grow. Over the next month or so, Hannah had become friends with Dave and Tim as well.

Ashley had another checkup with her doctor the first part of February and the doctor put her on bed rest for the duration of her pregnancy. After a week of bed rest, she was starting to drive Tim crazy, so she asked Sarah if she could stay with her for a little while. Tim had started volunteering at the homeless shelter three days a week and felt it would be wrong of him to stop doing such. It was actually his idea for Ashley to call Sarah. Sarah explained that she would love the company, telling Ashley to pack her bags and come on. Ashley stayed with Sarah, Brandon, Hannah, and Ryan until the week before Sarah's wedding to Dave. That is when Ashley's water broke.

Sarah rushed Ashley to the hospital and notified Tim and Dave. Dave was at the hospital within 10 minutes, while it took Tim the normal hour to drive from home. After Tim arrived, he found the labor and delivery room Ashley was in. Their doctor was just about to leave as Tim entered the room. He told Tim that the babies were on their way but probably would not be there until morning sometime. She had not fully dilated and was only at about four centimeters. That night, Tim stayed with Ashley in her room getting very little sleep. Her contractions had begun to increase in severity and frequency. The next morning, the doctor came in to check on her and decided it was time. The first baby was starting to crown. An hour later, Tim was standing at the nursery window with Sarah and Dave as they placed two beautiful girls in bassinets with little name cards next to them. Sarah Jean and Marilyn Rae were both introduced to their Aunt Sarah and Uncle Dave. Brandon had stayed home with Hannah and Ryan for the time being. They would bring him up later that day to meet his new cousins. Ashley would stay in the hospital one more day before getting released.

Sarah spent a lot of time that week at Ashley's house watching the children, giving Ashley and Tim a chance to rest. Sarah's wedding day was approaching fast. The day of Sarah's wedding came and Ashley helped her get dressed as the guests arrived. Tim showed them the way to the pond and had them take their seats. Dave's parents had divorced when he was a small child and had remarried since then, when they arrived, they were cordial to each other. They each brought their new spouses to the wedding and Dave was happy to see his step-mother and step-father as well as his parents. The wedding went exceptionally well and the reception was inside a large tent the decorator had set up. They all danced, drank, and had a merry ole time. After the reception, Dave and Sarah changed clothes and headed to the airport for their honeymoon in Hawaii. They left Brandon at home, asking Hannah to care for him during their absence for a week. Hannah was enjoying playing the role of mommy to Brandon and it made her start thinking about having children of her own.

When Sarah and Dave returned from their honeymoon, they found Hannah there alone with Brandon. There was no sign of Ryan. Sarah figured he was either in class or at work, but when he did not show the next day, she knew she had to talk to Hannah about his whereabouts. Sarah found Hannah in her room and asked her about Ryan.

"We got into a fight over something stupid, two days after your wedding, and he left," Hannah began saying.

"What was the fight about?" Sarah asked gingerly as they sat on Hannah's bed.

"He wanted sex, but Brandon was up playing in his room. I didn't want him to accidentally walk in on us, so I told Ryan not right then. I even said I would try that night, but that I did have a headache at the time. He said it was his right as a husband to get sex anytime he wanted, and then we started yelling at each other. That's when he walked out. He came back the next day, and we talked for a while, then he started demanding sex again. This time, when I refused, he slapped me telling me I was a poor excuse for a human being. I got up and literally threw him out. I packed his stuff and delivered it to him at his parents' house. That's the last I have seen or heard from him," she said, trying to be stoic.

"I will kill him. You never hit a lady," Dave said with anger from the doorway. He then entered the room and held both of them in his arms.

Over the next few hours, they moved to the living room and talked the situation over on the couch. Dave offered his service as an attorney, free of charge, but said they needed to try counseling first.

"It's no use," Hannah said. "He has already gotten a new girlfriend and moved in with her. He told me we were through and to file for divorce. On top of all that, I went to the doctor yesterday and found out that I am pregnant. I have been having morning sickness for the last month or so. I am about twelve weeks pregnant."

As she said this, she broke down in tears. Sarah held her, giving her comfort and motherly love. The next day, Dave filed for divorce on Hannah's behalf.

As the weeks went by, Hannah and Sarah talked about the options Hannah had with her pregnancy. Hannah quickly ruled out abortion, saying she felt that it was wrong. She wanted to at least deliver the baby into this world, after that, she would like to keep her child like Sarah had. She knew it was going to be hard, but she was willing to put forth the work.

Dave informed Hannah that her appearance in the divorce case would be the following Monday, and prepped her on what to say and how to act. Dave was not sure that Ryan was even going to show up, but knew he had been served paperwork. Ryan was back living at his parent's house after his new girlfriend had kicked him out. It seemed that Ryan felt sex was more important than anything else. During the time apart, Hannah had found out that Ryan had gotten fired for sexual harassment and had quit going to college due to his low grades. Dave was asking for $300 a month in child support and another $300 a month in alimony, knowing he could get the child support order, but not sure about the alimony. Dave was going to bury Ryan in debt for the next eighteen years or so.

In court, was the first time Ryan found out that he was going to be a father and cursed the judge for suggesting such a thing. He became obstinate and swore that she was a whore, yelling that the bastard was not his. He could get 10 guys that say they slept with her. Dave let him dig his hole deeper with every breath, so did the judge. When Ryan stopped ranting and raving, the judge granted the divorce and both the alimony and child support. The judge added that if he did not pay, he would spend time in city jail, and that once the baby was born, they would do a paternity test to be sure. The payments were to start immediately. On the way out of court, Ryan's father told him that he fucked up something good this time, as he slapped him in the back of the head.

Eight weeks after they were married, while at work, Dave got confirmation that the adoption of Brandon had been approved. He called Sarah asking her, Brandon, and Hannah to go out to dinner that night. He had some good news to share. Sarah agreed to have everyone ready that night at 6 p.m., throwing in that she had some good news also to share.

Dave got home, cleaned up, and got ready to go out to eat, everyone else was already ready. He drove to Rusty's and they got seated. While they waited to place their order, Dave told them his good news. Brandon finally had a father. They all clapped and Brandon gave him a hug.

"Now, what's your news?" Dave asked Sarah.

"Well, we went to the doctor today and Hannah found out the sex of the baby. It's a boy!" Sarah said joyfully.

"Congratulations, Hannah," Dave said interrupting Sarah.

"That's not all," Sarah continued.

"Twins?" Dave asked.

"Sort of. . ." Sarah continued nervously.

"Sarah is pregnant." Hannah chimed in during the awkward pause. "You're going to be a father."

As this news was sinking in, the server came to the table congratulating Dave on what he had just over heard. They order their meal as Dave tried to comprehend the fact that he was going to have a child of his own. Not that he didn't love Brandon, but his own flesh and blood child was on its way.

"Have you told Ashley ad Tim yet?" he asked.

"No, the only people that know now are at this table and our server," Sarah stated.

"After dinner, let's go over to their house and let them in on the good news," Dave stammered, still in shock and disbelief.

Once they got to Ashley and Tim's house, they broke the good news about Hannah's baby being a boy. Dave could not stop smiling as Hannah told them about the adoption of Brandon being complete. Then it was Dave's turn to take center stage. Before he could talk, he cleared his throat and pulled out two cigars, asking Tim to step out back with him. As they headed towards the back door, Dave knew Sarah would tell Ashley the good news. Tim grabbed a couple of beers for them out of the refrigerator. Once seated on the patio, Dave lit one of the cigars, handing the other to Tim, cracked open his beer, and told Tim his good news. Tim let out a whoop that the ladies and Brandon heard inside. They stayed for about an hour, then said it was getting close to Brandon's bed time and left.

Over the next week, they made plans for their Fourth of July camping trip. This time, they invited Hannah. She was starting to feel like part of the family and said she would love to go along with them. She had never been camping before and looked at it as a new adventure. She asked a thousand questions that she already kind of new the answers to like: Is there going to be a fire? Will we roast hot dogs? Can we make s'mores? Sarah explained the tradition and the fireworks that would be at the campsite. She said that Hannah might have a little difficulty sleeping in a tent, due to her growing belly. Hannah reassured Sarah that she wanted to try and thought she was going to enjoy camping very much. Hannah then thanked Sarah for all she had done over the last six months for her and started to cry.

Hannah had never told Sarah much about her parents, but felt the time was right to do so now. Brandon was at the park with Dave, and they would be gone for a few hours, so she knew she had the time.

"My parents never loved me. I was always a constant reminder of why they had to get married. They met in college and dated for a few months, then my mother found out she was pregnant. Her father made my dad marry her, and they resented each other ever since. My parents were never in love with each other and that showed throughout my childhood. My father would disappear for a night or two every week and mom knew he was seeing other women. Hell, Dad admitted as much to her several times. Grandpa told my dad that if he ever got a divorce, he would personally kill him, and I believe he would. My mother also was stepping out on dad except she always did it when he was at work. Mom smokes a lot of weed to try to forget about things and has forgotten me on several occasions. Although my father never hit me, he was and still is very abusive to my mother and me. When I told them about Ryan proposing to me, they told me that marriage was the best way to fuck up your entire life. My mother actually told me that marriage led to having a 'damn brat always around.' Her words not mine. As I started developing into a young woman, my father would accidentally rub against my chest. I even caught him trying to look at me in the shower on several occasions. I have never told anybody this before. I was kind of glad they kicked me out and really happy you let me stay here. I owe you so much, I know I will never be able to repay you fully." Hannah spoke with tears in her eyes and a lump in her throat.

Sarah held and comforted her for the better part of an hour, knowing some of this was memories and some was her hormones. When the boys returned, Hannah gave each of them a big hug and a kiss on the cheek, telling Dave thank you. He was dumbfounded. Over the next few weeks, Hannah and Brandon got more excited about the camping trip, so much so, that neither one of them could sleep the night before.

Like the previous year, they went swimming in the pond. This time, Ashley stayed near the shallow shores with Sarah Jean and Marilyn Rae with Hannah helping to watch the little girls.

"She was going to make a great mother," Sarah thought to herself as Hannah played with Sarah Jean.

The girls already had different personalities, as well as full heads of hair. Sarah Jean had strawberry-blonde like her mother and Marilyn Rae had black hair like her father. Both girls liked to play in the water, but neither would float. Sarah Jean was a daddy's girl and Marilyn Rae a mommy's girl. Tim was the only one able to soothe Sarah Jean when she was crying, no matter how hard Ashley tried, and vice versa with Marilyn Rae. Ashley spent about a half hour in the pond then got into the shade of the trees so she would not burn this year, taking the girls and Hannah along.

That night, they had hot dogs, to Hannah's delight, and made s'mores before the fireworks. Hannah and Brandon went through two boxes each of sparklers before the show. They all enjoyed their time that night. Hannah got a tent to herself and Sarah, Dave, and Brandon shared a tent. Ashley, Tim, and the girls slept in the largest one together. They all slept soundly that night. The next morning, Ashley cooked breakfast for everyone with Sarah's help. They ate and Hannah thanked Ashley and Tim for the great experience.

That next week was the opening of the new wing of the homeless shelter. After some deliberation, they had named it the Mark Edmonds building in remembrance of Ashley's late husband. Not only did it house 150 beds, it also held 150, one-bedroom transitional living apartments for the homeless, bringing the total to 250 beds and 150 transitional living apartments. They all went to the grand opening that following Monday morning and cut the ribbon to signify that it was open for business.

During the grand opening, the president and CEO of the shelter, Mr. James Jones, pulled Tim aside and offered him a full time position as the manager of daily living. The pay was more than he had been making with the other company, and he told them that he would have to discuss it with his wife. He would let them know in a day or two. He told Ashley about the offer over lunch that day, and she thought it would be a great opportunity for him, but left the decision up to him totally. She said she would be on board with him either way. That night, he slept on it, tossing the pros and cons of returning to the workforce. He knew Ashley needed help around the house with the twins, but also knew that she could always get the help from Sarah and Hannah. He knew it was an hour drive from home, but also knew he missed working.

The next morning, he made his decision. He would take the job and told Ashley about it over breakfast. She was both concerned and pleased with his decision but backed him 100 percent. That afternoon, he drove to the shelter's offices and informed Mr. Jones that he would accept the position. Mr. Jones told him that he could start the first of August.

Tim was thankful that he had left his resume with the human resources department earlier that year and drove home to tell Ashley. On his way, he made a pit stop by Dave's office, first telling him the good news. Dave invited him and Ashley out for supper that night and said he would not tell Sarah. He would let Tim do that over dinner. Tim agreed and told Ashley about everything when he got home. She was pleased with the job and happy about going to dinner with her dear friends to celebrate.

# Chapter 4

The rest of July seemed to fly by as Hannah started getting ready to go back to school that fall. It was going to be her senior year, and she was going to have a baby in just a few short months. Her due date was October 16 and it was quickly approaching. That year, she would become a student teacher in the first semester, having already passed the requirements and tests. She would be student teaching first grade at the same school Brandon would be going to the following year. She had applied that spring, taking some classes over the summer semesters, and was thinking about going for her master's degree in education in the evenings. She was working hard to fulfill her dream and was on track to do so. With Sarah's generosity and Dave's help, she was able to overcome the obstacles that popped up in her life. She knew the major obstacle had been Ryan, who had still not sent any of the court ordered money to her, even though she knew he had gotten a job as general labor at a local construction company. He was already $2500 dollars in the arrears. She also knew she would be seeing him in court again for the paternity test results once the baby was born. She knew whom she had slept with, and it was only one person, Ryan.

As she returned to school that fall, she was definitely showing and looked like she could deliver on any day. She had a doctor's appointment the day before school started and got a clean bill of health. The baby was progressing well and was right on track. Her lower back was starting to hurt more with each passing day. In her first night class, a young man named Austin sat next to her in the lecture hall, and she could tell he was smitten with her beauty. Not only could she tell by the way he looked at her, but he told her so as he asked if she was married. After class, she explained the situation to him in full detail, and he immediately asked her out. This happened in a couple of her classes with different young men, and she told them all they would have to wait until after her baby was born. That same day, she started her student teaching job.

Hannah left the house that morning and did not make it home until late that night. When she did get home, she was exhausted. She grabbed a light meal and went straight to bed. That continued for the next few days. On Thursday, Sarah caught her early in the morning and wanted to talk to her about something important.

"I have been doing some research and have found a facility that checks paternity before the baby is born. If you want, I can schedule you an appointment next week and get the results back in as little as three days. I will pay for it, but Dave will charge it to Ryan in court. How does that sound to you?" Sarah said quickly, knowing that Hannah did not have much time to waste.

"Okay, that sounds like a plan. You know my work and school schedule so a Monday or Friday would be best for me," Hannah said rushing out the door.

That day, Sarah made the call and actually got an appointment for the next Friday during the kids' lunch hour. She called the school and got the message to Hannah. Hannah had a week to get a hold of Ryan and have him there so they could get his DNA also. That chore was actually pretty easy as he was going to night school also. Although they had no classes in common, they were in the same hallway frequently. He actually was cordial when she stopped him and gave him the news. He said he would be there and he was. The procedure to test paternity took less than 15 minutes and Hannah was back to work before the lunch hour was up. Sarah knew that Hannah had only been with one man, and she knew Ryan was the father, but she was concerned all weekend about the results. Finally, the results came in on Wednesday.

When the results arrived, Sarah called Hannah on her cell phone and let her know. She also let Dave know. Dave then filed for the court to determine the paternity, a modification to child support and added the cost of the test to the paperwork. He saw the judge early the next day and informed him of everything that was going on, including that Ryan had a job and was not paying child support or alimony. The judge remembered the 'hot-headed punk' that had been in his courtroom earlier that year and put the case on fast track. The court date was set for the last week of September. Hannah's due date was closing in fast.

In court, Ryan thought his troubles were over, but they had just begun. Ryan's general laborer job paid almost $3000 a month and the court had gotten a copy of his pay stubs.

"Go fuck yourself, I ain't paying shit and you can't make me," Ryan told the judge when he read the results that Ryan was the father.

That got Ryan 30 days in city jail. It also got a garnishment of his wages adding up to $700 a month for current and past child support and another $300 for alimony. Ryan did get custody of the baby on the weekends, starting Friday night going until Sunday night. Ryan's father was so pissed at Ryan for opening his 'damn mouth,' that he actually slapped him across the face. Ryan was learning fast to shut the hell up and not talk to the judge like that. As Hannah left the courtroom, they were taking Ryan out in handcuffs to start his 30 days in jail.

That night, her water broke. She spent 14 hours in labor and Sarah sat with her through it all, while Dave stayed home with Brandon. Once the baby was born, they all came to the hospital, including Ashley, Tim, and the twins. He was a beautiful baby boy, weighing 7 pounds and 3 ounces. He was born with a full head of light brown hair and looked just like Hannah. Sarah asked Hannah if she had picked out a name yet and Hannah said yes.

"I was thinking of naming him after your brother and Dave, but not sure how you would feel about it," Hannah said shyly.

"I would be honored and so would Dave," Sarah replied.

"Then his name is going to be Mark David Shelton," Hannah stated with cheer.

Everyone, except Hannah, was looking through the glass of the nursery, as they brought Mark David in and laid him in the crib wearing a little blue hat. They all cheered and Ashley began to cry knowing that he was named after her late husband. Hannah had wanted to thank the people in her life that meant the most to her and felt this was a perfect way to include everyone. He was born three weeks early, but Hannah was able to leave the hospital the next day with her bouncing baby boy in tow.

Sarah had a sonogram scheduled the next morning to find out the sex of her baby, so she and Dave went early. The doctor started the sonogram shortly thereafter. Sarah heard the baby's heart beat and saw the little face before finding out she, too, was going to have a boy. Her due date was set for the same day as Brandon's birthday in January. Hannah thought it would be cool to have two children born on the same day five years apart and hoped it worked out that way. Sarah, on the other hand, thought it might cause hard feelings for one or the other as they grew up. She knew Brandon would want the spotlight on his birthday this year and hoped for everything to work out.

Hannah was given maternity leave from her student teaching job, about three months. She did not have to return to work until the end of the winter break, January 5th the following year. Sarah and Dave talked to her professors getting her assignments and learning materials for the next month. Hannah could take some time off and spend it with her new baby boy.

As Halloween approached, Ashley and Tim talked to Sarah and Dave about their trick-or-treating plans. It was decided that they would all go again this year, including the twins, Hannah, and her new baby, after all they thought of Hannah as part of the family. She had been unofficially adopted and would remain so until the day she died. Sarah and Dave told this to Hannah as they invited her to go with them on Halloween night. She was overjoyed that she had found a loving and caring family to be a part of. She only wished it hadn't taken her 20 years to find them. Hannah often wondered what it would have been like to grow up as a younger sister to Sarah. She had learned a lot about Mark from both Sarah and Ashley; she believed he would have been a wonderful brother. She wished she could have met him and spent time with such a loving and caring man. She knew that Sarah was loving and caring and knew that Mark, even if he was only half as caring, would have been a thousand times better than what she knew growing up.

Even though there was little sexual abuse in her family, the mental abuse was there all the time. Her father calling her a mistake or telling her that her mother should have gone to the clinic to get the abortion did not really help to improve her family dynamics. The family Hannah was from was dysfunctional to say the least and her father resented her and blamed her for ruining his life. On numerous occasions, he would tell her that he had been a ladies' man and could get any girl he wanted until her mother got pregnant.

Ashley had thrown her a baby shower the weekend before Hannah had given birth. Hannah had gotten a lot of cute outfits for herself and the baby, but the biggest gift was a combined gift from all of them. They paid off her student loans and gave her an additional $250,000 to continue her education, or whatever she wanted to do with the money. They just had one request—not to move out of Sarah's house. Sarah insisted that she was another sister in the family.

Hannah started receiving her child support and alimony payments on the third of November. That year, they had four extra mouths for Thanksgiving: Hannah, her baby, and the twins. They wound up cooking six turkeys and made sixteen casseroles, taking the majority of them to the homeless shelter. They ate their Thanksgiving dinner at the shelter as Tim introduced them to the staff and some of the longtime residents he had gotten to know. They all felt good helping the less fortunate at the shelter, and Hannah even inquired about either a volunteer or a part-time position. At that time, they did not have any available part-time positions, but she was told she could volunteer if she wanted. Although it was not for long, she knew what it was like to not have a home and wanted to help others like she had been helped. She started volunteering during her free time from work and school.

That Christmas, they all gathered at Ashley's house on Christmas Eve. It was planned that they would all stay the night and have Santa Claus accidentally be seen by Brandon. Tim would play the role as the others pretended to sleep. That night, everything went off without a hitch and Brandon saw the big man placing presents under the tree. Santa then ate a cookie and then disappeared out the back door, leaving Brandon at the top of the stairs in shock and awe. Brandon ran into the room. His parents were supposedly sleeping in and he was yelling so loud he woke everyone up including the babies. The next morning, they opened their presents and ate a wonderful breakfast thanks to Ashley and Hannah. Sarah was on baby duty that morning and could not help cook for the guys.

They gathered at Sarah's house for New Year's Eve and allowed Brandon to try to stay up with them this year. They talked and ate over dinner, then moved to the living room for coffee and beers. Brandon had three cups of hot chocolate before 10 p.m. and was snoring by 11 p.m. At ten minutes to midnight, Sarah woke him up so he could ring in the new year with them. He felt like a such a little man as he watched the ball drop in New York City. After the Ball dropped, he fell back asleep on the couch and Dave carried him to his room for the night.

As Sarah's due date quickly approached, they all were getting excited. Ashley and the twins spent most days at Sarah's house while Tim was working at the shelter. One day, while Ashley was over, Sarah Jean said her first word, "Mama." Both Ashley and Sarah looked at each other in disbelief. Hannah came home from work for lunch that day and was told about Sarah Jean talking. She was sorry that she had missed it by mere minutes.

On her way back to work, Hannah decided to stop at the local florist to have some flowers delivered to Sarah, just to show her appreciation of Sarah. While at the florist's, she ran into Austin, who remembered her from class last semester. They started up a conversation and talked for about 10 minutes. It turned out, that his family owned the florist, and he was working there while in college. He, too, was studying to be a teacher and was in his senior year of studies. Before she placed the order for the flowers, he asked for her phone number, so they could keep in touch and then asked her for a date. She explained that it would be difficult to date with her baby at home, but gave him her number. She added that he could call her that night after class if he wanted to.

He called her right at 10 p.m. that night, and they talked for about half an hour before she said she needed to get some sleep. Again, Austin asked her to go out that coming Saturday. She said she would think about it and get back to him by Wednesday. On Tuesday morning, she told Sarah about Austin and the offer to go on a date that weekend. Sarah was overjoyed by this prospect and told her to go for it but to remember the three simple rules.

That night, she talked to Austin again for about 30 minutes, telling him that she was still thinking about the dating situation. She told him that if she said yes there were going to be some ground rules, and then told him about the three simple rules that Ashley had originally started. He was okay with them and agreed that they were a great idea. She enjoyed talking to Austin and thought he was a handsome guy. She knew she liked him a little more than friends and thought that she would date him. First, she wanted to see how patient he could be, so she was dragging out her answer. She again told him to call her the next night for an answer.

On Wednesday, he happened to see her in one of the hallways at college and made small talk for a few minutes. Before they went their own ways, she reminded him to call her that night. He called her at 10 o'clock on the dot, and this time they talked for 45 minutes, before he again asked her out for Saturday. This time she said yes, but it had to be during the day over lunch or in the early afternoon. She told him that she had to spend time with her son and wanted to be home Saturday night. He accepted this compromise and agreed to meet her at the Pizza King, just off the college campus, for lunch. She said she would be there and told him good night.

As she hung up the phone, she started questioning herself about dating while having a baby so young. She thought about canceling the date with Austin and decided to talk to Sarah about it in the morning. The next morning, Sarah understood her concerns and suggested that she go ahead with the date, as it was a friendly date, and she was young. She did not want to see Hannah be lonely like she had been until she met Dave. And she did not want Hannah to sleep around with every Tom, Dick, and Harry that came by. She knew the urges Hannah had to be having even though she had recently given birth. She had them also after the birth of Brandon and knew she had needed help to control them. Ashley had been that lifeline and had gotten her the extra help she needed. Now it was her turn to help Hannah, even though she did not have an addiction to sex.

That Saturday, Hannah packed up Mark David and went to the Pizza King. She arrived a few minutes late, not having the experience of being a parent and hauling a baby around. Austin was already there, thinking he might have been stood up, as she entered with her baby in tow. They ordered a large pepperoni pizza and sat in a corner booth while it was cooking. Austin asked Hannah what she did at the homeless shelter, and she explained that right now, she just did whatever needed to be done. She had told him about volunteering there on one of their previous phone calls, and he seemed really interested in it at the time. She was sure he would forget, but he hadn't and even asked her how to volunteer himself. She told him about Tim and said she would talk to him about it. Austin seemed to like the fact that she had brought her baby, and he even seemed to like holding Mark David. When Mark David began to cry at feeding time, it was Austin that fed him his bottle.

That night, she talked to Tim, not only about Austin but also about helping out by offering free tutoring sessions to anyone who wanted it. She knew there were children and adults that needed help with reading and basic math, she felt it was right to pass on the knowledge she had. She thought weekends would be a great time for her to do that, and he liked the idea. Tim said he would talk to his superiors on Monday and see what they could work out. She even told Austin about this ingenious idea over the phone, as they talked late into the night. He thought it was a great idea and informed her he, too, would love to help with that project. He told her to let him know when and if they could get started.

That following Tuesday, Tim was at Sarah's house waiting for Hannah to come home. He had some great news for her. When she walked in, she hugged him and said it was a wonderful surprise to see him that night. He asked her to take a seat, that he wanted to talk to her, and asked Sarah and Dave to join them. They sat at the kitchen table as Sarah put on some coffee for everyone.

"Do you remember your idea about tutoring at the shelter?" he asked without letting her answer. He continued, "Well, I have bad news and good news about that. First, they will not let you volunteer as a tutor, something about logistics and legal issues. They are willing to pay you and up to three others to do the tutoring for a few hours both Saturday and Sunday, but the catch is, no one can tutor more than 10 hours a week, and they have to be in their senior year of college at least. The pay would be $12 an hour paid biweekly on Fridays. How does that sound to you?"

"That sounds great. I already have at least one other person wanting to tutor and maybe a couple of others in my classes would like the opportunity. It won't be much money, but the experience would be worth it. Thank you, Tim. I have to call Austin and tell him the good news," Hannah said gleefully.

"Wait a minute. There is something else I need to tell you," Tim said quickly. "You will be the supervisor of the tutoring program and will have to hire the tutors yourself."

With that, Hannah grabbed her cell phone and dialed Austin to tell him the good news. Before hitting send, she asked how soon they could start.

"As soon as you hire some tutors. This weekend would be fine," Tim stated.

She told Austin the good news and was very excited about the prospect to add this to his resume. He asked her to stop by the florist first thing in the morning, and he would fill out the application and get it back to her that night at school. Now she had to find two more tutors, if possible, but knew it might take a while. When she got to school that night, she sent out a few feelers to some of her friends. One said that she would think about it, but the homeless were always dirty and smelled. Another flat out said no way would he help the slobs. Austin caught her between classes and asked for another application because he, too, had been telling others about this opportunity and had someone interested. He explained that a guy in one of his ESL classes, Bradley, had been looking for part-time work on the weekends and thought it sounded like a good idea to help the less fortunate. Bradley was bilingual as was Austin. Austin spoke fluent Spanish; Bradley spoke Russian and Croatian. Hannah knew the different languages would come in handy at the shelter from her previous volunteering there. Austin got the second application and asked her to meet him after class. She agreed and they went their ways for now.

After classes were over that night, Austin and Hannah met up at Pizza King for a pizza and to talk. Bradley came in a few minutes later, and they had him sit with them. Bradley was a nice-looking young man and thanked Hannah personally for the chance to earn some extra money on the weekends. They discussed the work schedule at the shelter, deciding a split shift would work best. This way, they would not interfere with the lunch schedule at the shelter. Hannah called Tim to verify that would be acceptable, and he thought it would be perfect. The only thing left to do was to get the applications turned in the next morning. They finished their meal and went their own ways for the night. Hannah slept well that night with dreams of helping the homeless.

That Friday, Tim called and said everyone was added to payroll. The time of the tutoring session had been set and announced to the residents. Some of the residents already showed interest in wanting to learn. Hannah told Austin and Bradley that night over pizza, and they were excited to start the next day. They decided to make a lunch date. The three of them had a two-hour window between tutoring sessions, therefore, deciding that the best place for the lunch date was Pizza King. It was about 10 minutes from the shelter, and they could ride together alternating drivers and cars. Austin claimed the first day and Bradley volunteered for Sunday.

That first day they had 18 school-aged children and five adults come to them for tutoring. The children wanted to get better grades so when they grew up, they would not be in this situation with their families. Most of the adults just needed help with reading and writing, so they could fill out applications for work. That day, they were busy, but was able to help all of them. They broke the children up by educational levels and taught them as a class instead of one-on-one tutoring. If one needed the extra help, they got it. Bradley helped the adults that morning and Austin helped them after lunch. Both also helped Hannah with the children. At four that day, they decided to get dinner together and talk about their experiences. To celebrate their achievements, they went to Rusty's for a good meal. Hannah ordered a salad and the guys ate burgers. They gave each other kudos as they ate and laughed together. It went about the same on Sunday.

With the success of the weekend and the begging of the residents, the shelter agreed to allow more tutors to help out. That week, Hannah found a couple of people interested and so did Austin and Bradley. By the end of the first month of tutoring, they had grown to seven tutors. The original three still went to lunch daily at Pizza King and enjoyed each other's company greatly. That's when a new person popped into her life. Sarah had her baby on February 3rd. She named him Robert Eugene Palmer. He weighed in at 7 pounds and 12 ounces. Sarah's house was getting full and that's the way she liked it.

On weekends, when Hannah was gone to the shelter, Tim and Ashley usually came over to Sarah's house to visit. They would still be there when Hannah got home in the evenings. Now that Sarah had her baby, Hannah thought it might be a good idea to start taking Mark David to day care while she worked during the week. At night, she would bring him with her to class. On weekends, she could bring him to the shelter with her and give Sarah a break.

Hannah approached Sarah after she had been home from the hospital for about a week and asked her if she needed to find a place of her own. She could afford a small two-bedroom apartment for her and Mark David with the money she was now making. She would still be able to save most of the money she had been gifted. Sarah told her that she always had a place to stay, but if she wanted to be on her own, she would understand. Sarah also told her that she knew this day would come eventually but hoped Hannah would stay at least until she finished school. She was in her last semester and scheduled to graduate in June. Sarah then asked her to stay until she graduated and said she and Dave would buy her a house if she did. Sarah hated the thought of losing her and wanted to keep her close. The two women had become close friends and Sarah really liked her company. Hannah agreed not to look for anything until she at least graduated with her bachelor's degree.

Ashley had been taking classes online to become a daycare worker since the twins were born. She had already completed her bachelor's degree before her and Mark had married, so she only needed a few courses to gain her childcare professional certification. She easily completed the required courses and had gotten a job in a daycare to get the 720 hours of experience that she needed for her certification. She had kept this a secret from everyone, even Sarah. After Robert had been born, Ashley received her certificate and started applying for work in different day cares in the area. The first one to offer her a position was the shelter. It had been her first choice also. Not only did the shelter offer her a $25,000 salary, but also offered her free daycare for her children. Once she had been hired, she then told Tim, Sarah, and Dave over dinner that night. Sarah would inform Hannah that night, when she got home from school. Ashley was to start the first Monday in March.

Hannah was elated, when she heard the news about Ashley and called her to congratulate her personally. They talked for about an hour about school, working at the shelter, their children, and boys. They spent most of the time talking about Austin and Bradley both. It seemed that Hannah was starting to like Bradley a little more than Austin, but neither one of them knew this. She did not want to hurt Austin and wanted to remain friends with him, but not date him. Hannah told Ashley that they had never kissed and had only gone out on a couple of dates alone, otherwise Bradley had always been around. She asked for Ashley's advice, to which Ashley told her not to rush into anything and let things work themselves out. Ashley knew that both young men were nice from what Sarah had told her, but neither seemed quite right for Hannah and Ashley told her so. Her final advice was to just stay friends with both of them and if it was meant to be it will be.

Austin actually caught her that following Saturday morning and told her that he didn't think it was working out between them. He wanted to breakup, but remain friends. He told her that he loved her companionship as a friend. He admitted that he liked her, but was unsure about how she felt, and they were both still young enough to date others. He added that they could still go out, but only as friends. This both hurt Hannah and gave her some relief. She felt the same way.

As March approached, both Hannah and Austin started dating other people but would remain good friends. They still talked on the phone until late in the night, telling each other about their days and even their dates. Austin, at one point, even told her that Bradley had mentioned the possibility of dating her but did not want to step on anyone's toes. That next weekend, she flirted a little bit with Bradley to test the waters, so to speak. By the end of the second shift on Sunday, he had not only successfully gotten her phone number, but had also asked her out for the following Friday night.

Their date went pretty good at first, but during their date Hannah had remembered that she had forgotten to set the ground rules up with Bradley. She remembered when he leaned across the table and tried to kiss her near the end of their date. She quickly pulled away and explained the three simple rules to him. He said he understood the rules as she had stated them and apologized for his actions. He had not wanted to upset her, but inadvertently had. He asked her to give him one more chance for a first date, this time knowing the rules. She laughed and said yes. They went out the next night for their second first date.

She called Austin after their date on Friday night and told him all about the date and forgetting to tell him about the ground rules. They both agreed that they could not blame Bradley for doing something he did not know was wrong. She also told Austin about their upcoming date the next night and promised that she would call him afterwards.

Their second first date went well this time. Instead of trying to kiss her at the end, he simply hugged her goodnight. She told Austin over the phone that night that Bradley had been a complete gentleman. Austin and Hannah talked for about 45 minutes and then Bradley rang in.

She let Austin go and switched over to Bradley and talked to him for an hour before going to sleep that night. She was starting to get confused because she had feelings for Austin and Bradley both and did not want to hurt either one of them. She decided to go to Sarah and Ashley both for help in this situation. Ashley suggested that she keep it strictly platonic for a while with both of them. Sarah agreed.

# Chapter 5

At the end of March, Dave received a letter at his office with no return address. This was a little unusual and out of the norm for most of his clients. Upon opening and reading it, he thought it was just another piece of correspondence from an angry spouse, but it had a different tone entirely. It was too personal. It read:

> *Dear Fuckwad.*
>
> *You have ruined my life. You have stolen my money, caused me to get a criminal record, and now I am in the position to take control of the situation. You, that pretty little wife of yours, newborn baby, and child might want to watch out on your travels. I am not making a threat; I am making a goddamn guarantee. You have fucked with the wrong person this time you gutless bastard. You won't see me coming, but you better watch your fucking back. I am coming for you and that fucking slut of a bitch that you represent.*

There was no signature on the letter and no distinguishing markings. It appeared to have been typed on an old manual typewriter and was typed on plain copy paper. The address on the envelope had been typed also with the same machine it seemed.

At first, Dave did not think anything of the letter and set it aside for safe keeping. By the end of the week, he had gotten another letter addressed to "Dear Fuckwad." This time, it gave details about his and his wife's cars, details including where they are parked at night and what time he leaves for work daily. He kept this letter with the first one, although this time he informed Sarah about the letters. She knew he got hate mail occasionally, but it never included any details about her. She wanted him to call the police about the situation at hand, but he refused, saying there was nothing they could do at the time. He told her that he would keep the letters just in case something did happen, but that he was sure it was just someone blowing off steam. He felt nothing was going to happen.

Over the next few weeks, nothing out of the ordinary did happen, then a third letter arrived in the mail. This time to his home. The envelope was addressed to both him and Sarah and the letter inside was addressed to «Mr. and Mrs.

Fuckwad." This time, he noticed that the letter had been postmarked locally. The letter also included information about what they had been wearing a couple of days ago and how pretty Sarah had looked going into the supermarket that Tuesday.

Now Sarah was starting to get scared and insisted that they call the police and inform them. Dave concurred and dialed the cops. A patrolman was at their door less than a half of an hour later taking a report. He informed Dave and Sarah there wasn't much to go on at that time but that he would get extra patrol in the area just in case. Again, everything went back to normal for a week or so then the phone call came in.

The call came in on the house phone from a private number while Sarah was trying to put Robert down for a nap. She answered on the third ring and got a distorted voice telling her how beautiful she was. The distorted voice also told her that he watched her in her sleep and knew what nightgown she wore to bed. The voice told her not to call the police, nor inform Dave about the call, then abruptly disconnected. Sarah immediately called Dave to tell him. His house number was an unlisted number, and he could not figure out how this person had gotten it. He called the police from his office and made a report right there over the phone.

That night, they had plans to meet up with Tim and Ashley for dinner at Rusty's. Over dinner, Sarah told Ashley about the letters and the phone call. Sarah explained that she did not think anything was going to happen, but she was a little scared. Ashley agreed that she should be cautious not knowing what kind of person they were dealing with. The thing that bothered Sarah the most was that they had called her on the house phone. Nobody ever calls on that phone; they always use their cells.

After dinner, they all went back to Sarah's house to wait for Hannah to come home and informed her. Hannah didn't think it was anything more than a joke at first, but when they told her about the phone call, she knew it might be getting serious. Dave had stopped and gotten some pepper spray on his way to dinner that night and had given one to Sarah and Hannah while they were talking. He hoped that would be enough of a deterrent in case someone did try something. Sarah said she was going to start taking Brandon to and from school instead of having him ride the bus, knowing that he would not be happy with this. His safety was a priority for her.

More letters came in the mail two days after the phone call. This time, they were addressed to Dave's office and his house. It appeared that the letter had been copied and mailed to both locations. Both started out "Dear Fuckwad" and the author knew about their dinner with Ashley and Tim, what they had ordered, and what time they left the restaurant. They knew for sure someone had been watching them. What they did not know was who and why.

It was quiet for about a week, after that, Sarah and Dave had started to think another letter or phone call was coming shortly, but none did. Life seemed to resume its normalcy, and they began to forget about the harassment. Over the next few weeks, they began to think that the sick joke might be over until Sarah received a photo in the mail. It was not in an envelope, just a plain photo of her walking to her car. The photograph had a post-it note attached with "Damn you're hot" typed on it. Not sure if this was connected to the previous letters, she placed it in the waste bin in the kitchen. She called Dave and told him, and he suggested that she retrieve it and keep it just in case. Then everything went back to normal again.

By the beginning of June, they had forgotten about the letters and started to plan the Fourth of July party. They also were planning a surprise party for Hannah's graduation. Both parties were going to take place at Ashley and Tim's house. The first party, Hannah's party, was going to be on the day before her commencement ceremony, June 15th. Ashley had ordered streamers, a congratulations banner, all the food, and some wine. Tim and Dave would grill hot dogs and hamburgers, while the ladies would make shrimp cocktails inside. Ashley invited Bradley and Austin one day while she was at work when she put in a time off request. She explicitly told them not to let Hannah know.

The weekend before the surprise party, the supplies arrived and Ashley was busy setting everything up for that coming Tuesday. At the last-minute, Tim and Ashley decided to change the menu to shrimp kabobs with asparagus cooked on the grill to go with the shrimp cocktails the girls would be making. Ashley ran to the store in town to get more shrimp and the asparagus that she needed while Tim watched the twins. While she was on her errand, Marilyn Rae spoke to her father saying "Dada" and started to walk. Tim quickly grabbed his cell phone and started recording the progress. He sent a video of it to Ashley, Dave, and Sarah's cell phones. Ashley was extremely happy when she got the video, so happy that she dropped a dozen eggs that she was picking out, breaking them on the floor. Sarah immediately called Ashley to find out if she had seen the video yet, and they both cried happy tears over the phone.

When Ashley got back home, she was able to watch Marilyn Rae taking a few steps and falling on her butt in person. She was so excited, that she almost forgot the two bags of groceries in the back seat of her car. Sarah and Dave showed up at Ashley's house about 15 minutes after Ashley had gotten home to see this wonder for themselves. Sarah suggested they use this as an alibi to get Hannah over to the house for her surprise party.

The two couples sat around talking, while Brandon and the three smaller children played in the playroom. Hannah and Mark David were at the homeless shelter tutoring those in need, while the adults were working out the small details of her party. Tim and Dave drank a couple of beers and the ladies drank some wine. Around 3 p.m., Sarah and Dave started their return trip home and arrived just minutes before Hannah.

When Hannah walked in the house, Sarah showed her the video of Marilyn Rae and Hannah called Ashley right away to congratulate her. Neither Ashley nor Sarah let on about the upcoming party, but Ashley did invite Hannah over on Tuesday for a family get together.

Hannah agreed to going with Dave, Sarah, and the two babies around 10 a.m. Tuesday morning. Hannah was looking forward to seeing Ashley and Tim, but most of all, she was looking forward to seeing the twins again. It had been about two weeks since she had been able to play with them, and she was missing them something terrible. On Sunday morning, Sarah took a couple of gifts for Hannah over to Ashley's house and wrapped them while she was there. Tim and Dave had a guys' day planned that day. They were going to a car show, then to watch the Indy car race on television at Sarah and Dave's place. They were to be home around 2 p.m. Tim had driven to Sarah's house and met up with Dave for their man's day, stopping only for gas and to buy a 24-pack of beer. He believed that you never show up to someone's home empty-handed. Tim arrived at Dave's house, and as he was pulling into the driveway, his phone rang. He answered without looking at who it was that was calling.

"You are going to the car show with that Fuckwad," a distorted voice said.

"Who is this?" Tim demanded.

"Your worst nightmare," the voice replied. "Listen up, I have been watching all of you. I know when you sleep and when you take a shit. I am going to ruin all of your lives, like you ruined mine." Then the distorted voice abruptly disconnected the call.

After Tim realized that the caller had hung up, he looked to see what number it had come from.

"Damn, a private number," he stated in disbelief.

Tim informed Dave about the call as soon as Dave got in the truck. Dave cursed and informed Tim about the letters and phone calls they had gotten earlier. Since there was no direct threat to the ladies, they decided to not tell them about the phone call and headed for the car show.

That afternoon when Tim returned home, he told Ashley about the phone call.

"How did they get your number and why harass you?" was her first question.

"I don't have a clue," Tim replied dumbfounded.

When Hannah got finished with the tutoring session at the shelter, Ashley called her and asked her to meet them at Rusty's for dinner. She asked her to go home and cleanup first and be at the restaurant at 6:20 p.m. This would give Ashley and Tim time to get into town. What she did not tell her was the fact that it would give Ashley time to get a surprise together for all of them. She then called Sarah and asked her and Dave to bring the children with them. Ashley had been keeping this secret for about a month now and even Tim had no clue about it.

Ashley, Tim, and the twins were the first to arrive at the restaurant. They arrived at six fifteen and Ashley asked for a private room for 10 to 15 people. Tim knew something was up when Ashley made that request, but had no idea what it was. She went ahead and ordered three bottles of wine, a bottle of champagne, and two pitchers of beer when she requested the room.

"You do remember her party isn't until tomorrow, right?" Tim asked softly.

"I know, but I have something to give her that will not wait until tomorrow," Ashley said with a smile.

The curiosity was killing Tim, but he knew she would not divulge the surprise to anyone, until she was ready to. Sarah, Dave, and three children showed up first. Sarah told Ashley that she was giving Mommy Hannah a break tonight and was going to watch Mark David for her. Then she informed Ashley that Hannah had a bad day tutoring and would be there shortly.

"What is the special occasion?" Sarah asked.

"She won't tell anyone, but she has a gift for Hannah," Tim responded

"But the party isn't until. . .," Dave started to say.

"It's no use. She is the most stubborn when it comes to secrets," Sarah interjected.

Hearing this put an evil grin on Ashley's face, knowing there were never any truer words spoken. She could be mischievous and keep a secret so good, that a team of horses could not pull it out of her. Sarah had seen it before, when Ashley had first dated her brother Mark. She remembered the time that she saved up her money and bought concert tickets to some show and hinted to Mark about it for two weeks. She could not remember who was performing, but she did remember it was their third date. She also remembered that Ashley had only told her that she planned on kissing Mark that night. That was the first time Ashley had explained the three simple rules to her. Sarah's brother, Mark, had complained about always having to meet up in a public location with her after the first two dates. He had also asked Sarah why he had to meet Ashley at a 24-hour store off the college's campus that night, knowing the two of them were friends and talked about everything.

It wasn't until after they returned home, that Sarah found out what the secret had been and it took Mark telling her to get the information.

Sarah was sure whatever the surprise for Hannah was must be very important to Ashley and that she would not just keep any small secret from her. They had been friends for a long time now and told each other everything. Or, so she thought.

Hannah arrived at the restaurant and made her way to the private room. Once there, Ashley poured Hannah a glass of wine. After they ordered their meals, Ashley stood to speak.

"I propose a toast to the hardest working mother in the world. Hannah, you have had great obstacles thrown at you throughout your life and have fought to overcome them. Now you are graduating with a bachelor's in teaching on Wednesday, and as our friend, we wanted to congratulate you in a special way. All of us have come to love and adore you as a sister, but there comes a time that the baby bird needs to leave the nest. We, together, have gotten you a special gift and I have been elected to give it to you."

Ashley said these words, as she pulled a manila envelope out of her purse. She handed the envelope to Hannah and asked her to wait to open it until dinner was completed. Ashley knew this was going to drive everyone crazy with anticipation and it thrilled her even more. After their meals, Hannah asked if it was okay to open the envelope. Ashley grabbed the champagne as

Hannah opened the envelope. Inside, were two sets of keys and two titles—one to a new car and the other to a house. The confused look on Hannah's face told Ashley that she had better start explaining everything.

"I know your car still works, but I also know it costs a lot in upkeep. I bought you a new car and it is being delivered to your new house as we speak," Ashley stated matter of fact. "No, you don't have to move out of Sarah's house if you don't want to but you do have a home of your own three blocks away from her, if you so desire. Here in a minute, we all are going to go to see your new home and tomorrow you and I are going to order you some furniture for your house," she finished by opening the champagne.

The look on everyone's faces was priceless. The four adults were in total shock as Ashley smiled her little evil grin. She would later explain that she had gotten the idea from Sarah earlier that year and ran with it. When the house in Sarah's neighborhood came up for sale, she put in a good offer and got the house. She had gone into town the previous day by herself and bought the car and closed on the house, signing all the paperwork and planning the dinner at the same time. The only thing left to do was sign the title and deed over to Hannah and make them both officially hers.

When they got to the house, Hannah saw the new black Mustang in the driveway of a nice and large Tudor home. Ashley explained that there were five bedrooms with three bathrooms upstairs and a finished basement with an office space and a private bathroom along with a family room that could hold a large party downstairs. Hannah opened the door for the first time and walked in to check out the house. Upon entry, she noticed another manila envelope on the floor just in the entrance way with her name on it. She looked at Sarah and shrugged her shoulders. Sarah shrugged back as Hannah bent over and picked up the envelope. Upon opening it, Hannah saw a certified check for $1 million that came out of Ashley's account. Hannah's jaw just about hit the floor.

As they toured the house, Tim pulled Ashley aside and asked the question that was on everybody's mind.

"How... when... why did you do all of this?" Tim said in a state of shock.

"I wanted to do something special for Hannah and I had the means to do it. So, I did," Ashley stated flatly.

"But why say it is from all of us," Tim asked nervously.

"Because we all love her and want her to be able to make it in this world. Now come on, let's catch up with the rest of the group," she replied as she headed up the stairs towards the bedrooms.

Tim had not been fully satisfied with her answers, hoping Sarah could get more out of her that night over their nightly chat on the phone. If not, then he would try to get more information out of her tomorrow morning. Before they left Hannah's new house, Ashley retrieved the second set of keys to the new car from the mailbox and gave them to Hannah. That night, Sarah called her as usual and asked the same questions that Tim had asked her at Hannah's new house. This time, Ashley explained a little bit better.

"I came from nothing. When I went to college, I had to work while I was in school and tried to keep my grades up. I hardly had any extra money for food and ate a lot of Ramen Noodles. I actually decided to skip a few meals and save up some money to go see a concert before I met your brother Mark. Once you introduced us, I found out that he liked the same group and had to get two tickets for the show. I got the tickets in the cheap seats and enjoyed the concert. I guess you can say I fell into money and I understand where

Hannah is at this point in her life. I remember wishing that someone would help me out and felt that since I now have the means to help her out, that I would do so," Ashley stated in a matter-of-fact tone.

"Yes, I remember you telling me about that in college, but I am here to help both you and Hannah now. I will be getting the rest of my inheritance, about $70 million in about a week and wanted to give some back to you. How much was the house? At least I can pay you back for that," Sarah spoke in a caring and loving tone.

"It was almost $900,000, but I wanted to do something special for her and you. You took her in when she had nowhere to go and I gave her a place to call home," Ashley stated.

The two ladies talked for about another hour and had decided that Sarah would split the cost of the house and the furniture that they would be buying the next day with Ashley. Ashley also agreed to be at Sarah's house the next morning to pick up Sarah and Hannah and go furniture shopping. After the phone call, Ashley wrapped herself in her favorite blanket and drifted off to sleep.

She woke the next morning and decided to take a bath as usual. She knew Tim would sleep for about another hour before waking up and she simply relaxed for that time. After he awoke, she drained the tub and dried off as he climbed into the shower. She asked him if she could use the truck that day in case they found something that they could not get delivered. He agreed on one condition—that he came along to help lift the furniture. It was settled. The two of them would get the twins into daycare and go furniture shopping with Hannah and Sarah. Ashley already knew that Brandon and the babies were going to a private babysitter for the day and thought this was a good idea.

They wound up going to four different furniture stores that morning, in which Hannah did not see anything appealing to her taste. They decided to go to lunch and discuss what they had seen. Over their lunch break, Hannah explained that she really had no idea as to what she wanted in furniture. All she really cared about was a place to sit and a bed to sleep in. She explained, that she was a little overwhelmed by the two gifts she had received the previous night and was still kind of in shock. She expressed her appreciation of the wonderful gesture and all the help that they had given her, but did not know how to repay them for their generosity and probably never could. She explained that she felt in debt to each of them and did not like the feeling. She further explained that she would hardly ever be in that large house and did not feel right about them spending their money on her.

As soon as Hannah had finished explaining her feelings, Sarah spoke up and explained that they had unofficially adopted her into the family and that since she was a sister, she now had the family that loved her and had the money to lavish her with necessities. Sarah had just finished speaking when Ashley interjected that there was no need to repay them for anything. That it all was done in love. Then Ashley explained her experience in college and how hard it was to survive without anything. She further stated that she could not sit by and let her sister go down that road, if she could help it. Tim agreed and said he knew for sure that Dave would also agree.

They continued to talk as their meals arrived and found out that Hannah did like a sectional at one of the previous furniture stores. She also admitted that she likes either a light brown design or a floral print, but the sectional she had seen was a light gray. She further admitted that she was no interior decorator and was scared that she would get everything that clashed instead of flowed. By the time lunch was finished, they decided to get the sectional in the light gray and a bed for her. They would hire an interior decorator that afternoon to fill the house. Hannah liked this idea and asked if she could split the cost with them, explaining that she would enjoy being part of the experience instead of just receiving the gift. They all agreed to pitch in and Sarah started looking up interior design companies.

They then went back to the third furniture store and bought the sectional that Hannah had liked. They also got her a couple of beds, one king-sized and one queen-sized, both with beautiful matching head and foot boards. While they were there, Ashley suggested they find a bed for Mark David, as he would be growing fast and would need one soon. After picking out a bed for Mark David, Tim suggested they look at the televisions and entertainment systems. They found a nice entertainment center that would hold up to an 85-inch television that complimented the gray sectional. Then they found a nice 85-inch television and a sound system to go with it. As they were heading toward the register to complete their purchases, Hannah spotted a couple of rocker-recliners in the same gray color as the sectional and wanted to add them onto the list. Hannah thought that it would give guests a place to sit and Ashley agreed.

Hannah tried to purchase the items and Sarah beat her to the punch. Sarah paid for everything that afternoon, setting up home delivery for the following Monday. Hannah promised to pay her back and Sarah refused the gesture.

After the ladies and Tim were done buying the furniture, they decided to go to the Kitchen and Dining Rooms Plus store. Hannah had nothing at all to furnish a kitchen, let alone the huge one in her new home. Sarah and Ashley decided that this kitchen and dining room was to be one of a chef's dream. They all thought that the current kitchen appliances needed to go, so they ordered some top-of-the-line and stainless-steel appliances. The kitchen was L-shaped, with a huge island that sat six. It was an open concept kitchen that opened up to the dining room and living room. This was great because Hannah could keep an eye on Mark David and also visit with friends while entertaining. She got some really nice pots and pans, Hannah enjoyed cooking, so this set was perfect. They bought two sets of dishes, one for every day and one for entertaining. Hannah decided the set for entertaining would be the multi-color set. She wanted a bit of color in the dining room. The dining room was huge, large enough to have a farm table set that sat 12 and a matching hutch.

After they were done with their shopping, they decided to bring their purchases to Hannah's new house. That way, when it was time to set up the kitchen, everything would be there. Once inside, they got to talking about layouts that might work for the living room. They moved into the kitchen when Sarah said that the kitchen really needed to be updated. After all, they were buying new appliances, they should just redo the kitchen. Ashley agreed the kitchen needed some updating and was willing to pay for the changes. Kitchens are usually the most expensive room in the house to remodel, but Ashley felt it would be fine as it would only add equity to the home down the line. Sarah said since she was looking into an interior decorator, she might as well check out a general contractor also.

After all the shopping, they decided to go to Rusty's for dinner and called Dave to meet them there in about an hour and a half. On their way, they stopped by a bedding and bath store to set up those two areas. They found some light pink sheets and a light purple comforter for Hannah's new bed. They decided to decorate the master bathroom in seascape print towels and decor. They picked up some plain sky-blue towels for her to use after her showers and baths to go along with the guest towels, that would hang in the towel holders on the walls.

Once they arrived, Sarah saw Gina and said hello to her. Not only was Gina Middleton the Maître' D, but she also was married to Charles "Rusty" Middleton. Charles had gotten his nickname "Rusty" as a child due to his hair being a rusty red color.

"How have you been doing, Gina?" Sarah asked.

"I have been good up until last week. I got sick about a week ago with a summer cold and was out of commission for the week. It's hell getting sick at my age," Gina stated knowing that she was only about 20 years older than Sarah.

"We haven't seen you or Rusty here for a while and was hoping everything was alright with you," Sarah stated with genuine concern in her voice.

"We had taken a couple of months off to travel abroad and see the world. We decided to tour Italy and it was beautiful," Gina said with a smile.

"That is wonderful that you could take that trip," Ashley spoke up.

"Are you going to seat these nice people or make them stand in the doorway all night?" Charles "Rusty" Middleton walked up behind Gina and jokingly asked at that point.

"Uncle Rusty, how have you been?" Sarah asked after seeing him and giving him a big hug and a kiss on the cheek.

"I am doing good. I have only one more payment on the loan to your parents and the restaurant is all mine. The 30-year loan will be paid off in only 26 years. I still miss your parents, Sarah; I miss them dearly," he stated with a joyful heart.

Rusty had met her father in college, and they had been best friends ever since. Rusty had not come from money but did get a little help from his parents to pay for his schooling. Rusty had decided to go into culinary arts his last year or so of college and quickly became a well talked about chef. One day, after her parents had gotten married, he had asked her father for a loan to be able to open the restaurant that is now Rusty's. He had done all the research and found a tract of land where he wanted to build, but the banks would not give him the money he needed to build. Upon asking, Sarah's father insisted on giving him a $5 million loan for 30 years at only one percent interest. He had the papers drawn up by his lawyers the next day and a certified check cut the following day. Sarah's father even went as far as to recommend a contractor, who owed him a couple of favors. The contract was signed in the hospital while "Uncle Rusty" and Sarah's father awaited her recovery from her tonsillectomy on her fourth birthday.

Uncle Rusty had been in her life since before she was born and was still a close friend of the family. Not only that but his restaurant had the best food in town. On the weekends there was a usual wait of about a half an hour to 45 minutes to get seated. It had been featured in several national magazines and even on national television shows due to the high quality of the food.

They were seated and their server, a young man about Hannah's age named James, took their drink orders. James returned with their drinks and asked if they were ready to order. They all ordered the sirloin steak and baked potatoes, except Hannah, who asked for a side salad instead of a baked potato. As James left the table with their food order, Ashley suggested that Hannah talk to him because he was a "cutie pie." Hannah agreed with her and tried to think of how to start up a conversation with him.

Throughout dinner, she was able to find out that he was single and he had also just finished college. He would be actually walking the stage with Hannah on Wednesday night. She thought that would be a great time to have a friendly meet up with him. She informed him of this, and he agreed to meet her at the auditorium about a half hour before their commencement ceremony was to begin. That way, they could get to know each other a little bit and see if they hit it off or not. After dinner, James placed the bill on the table and handed a note to Hannah, which included his phone number. As they left the restaurant, Ashley started jokingly picking on Hannah about picking up a guy who was so yummy looking, causing Tim to roll his eyes.

Tim was not a jealous man, he knew Ashley loved him and was just joking with Hannah, but he thought she was taking it too far. He agreed that James had been a good-looking young man and hoped for the best between them, but he also tried to remind Hannah about the three simple rules that Ashley had created. As Tim drove them back to Sarah's house, Hannah actually texted James and gave him her number. That night James called Hannah, and they talked for a couple of hours before going to sleep for the night. She told James about Mark David and the three simple rules when he asked her for a date near the end of the phone call. He accepted both and said he thought the three simple rules were a good idea. He especially enjoyed the fact that she had a son and informed her he loved children. He also informed her that when he decided to get married, he wanted children of his own. He told her that he had Saturday night off, and she agreed to a date that Saturday night after her shift at the shelter. They decided to meet at the Pizza King, just off the college campus. He really did not want to return to his workplace on a date.

After dropping off Sarah and Hannah, Tim and Ashley went to the daycare and retrieved the twins. They arrived five minutes before the daycare closed and Ashley started apologizing for their lateness. The daycare staff explained that there was no need to apologize for they were great parents and the children could have stayed longer with just a phone call to inform the daycare staff. When Sarah and Hannah got home, Sarah paid the babysitter for the all-day job she had done and let the teenager go home. She first kissed Brandon goodnight and then each of the babies. She already was trying to get Mark David to call her Aunt Sarah, even though he could not talk yet. She thought to herself that she was going to miss him and Hannah when she did move to her own house, yet she knew they were always welcome at her house anytime. She also knew that she would be going to see them both on playdates and she would frequent Hannah's home.

The next morning, Ashley got up and took her normal bath before setting up for the surprise party for Hannah. When Tim awoke, he went to town and got a few supplies they had forgotten and also picked up more food for the cookout that day. Sarah, Hannah, Austin, and Bradley were supposed to be at Ashley's house that afternoon. Ashley had a lot to do that morning, getting the banner hung and ready for the party, so much so that she did not think she would be able to complete it all before everyone arrived. She decided to kick it into high gear and had completed the decorations and everything by noon that day, giving her a few minutes to rest before Bradley arrived.

Austin had arrived right on time with a bottle of wine, a bottle of champagne, and some flowers for Hannah. He told Ashley that he loved her house and asked about the possibility of playing with the twins a little bit before the party started. She told him that would be okay and that they would enjoy some playtime in the living room. Ashley felt like she had been abandoning the twins that day because she had been so busy getting everything set up for the party. Tim arrived back home just as Austin was walking in the front door. He quickly grabbed the bags out of the back of his pickup. He knew he was running late, but he had a hard time finding everything for the cookout. He actually had to go to several stores to find the shrimp and asparagus. He had also grabbed some beer for everyone if they wanted it.

Ashley was glad to see Tim pulling into the driveway as she let Austin in the house. She knew that he would help her relax a little bit before Sarah and Hannah arrived. As Tim set the groceries and few party favors on the counter in the kitchen, Ashley was pouring herself a glass of wine. Tim offered Bradley and Austin a drink, and they both asked for a beer. Tim informed them that there was a strict two drink limit because they did not want anyone to drive drunk after the party. Tim had placed some sun tea in a carafe before he had left the house that morning and poured himself a glass after he passed out the beers. Dave arrived about five minutes before Hannah and Sarah, explaining that he had to do some filing at the office that morning and it had taken a little longer than he thought it would. Ashley directed him to the backyard where Tim was starting up the grill drinking his iced tea.

"Got any lemon for the tea?" Dave asked as he exited the back door of the house.

"Yeah, I have it in the cooler along with the beers," Tim said with a laugh.

The two guys sat on the Adirondack chairs on the back patio as the shrimp kabobs and the asparagus were cooking, just talking about nothing important. When Sarah and Hannah arrived, they heard the cheers inside and went in to congratulate the graduate. Ashley started by handing out the shrimp cocktails and asked how long the rest of their lunch would be. Tim said it would take the shrimp and asparagus about another five minutes to cook, then it would be time to eat. Once the kabobs and asparagus were ready, they all ate on the back patio. Some of them sat at the picnic table, others in the Adirondack chairs.

After they finished their meals, Ashley excused herself and gathered all the gifts for Hannah, bringing them out to the porch for her to open them. Hannah received a brand-new laptop computer from Sarah and Dave, along with several programs for it like Microsoft Office among others. Tim and Ashley gave her a Chromebook that she could take to class with her as she taught in the public school system. Bradley had given her a subscription to her favorite teaching magazine and Austin gave her the flowers. She enjoyed each and every gift and thanked them all for their generosity. Austin asked where Mark David was and Hannah explained that he, Brandon, and Robert Eugene were at Sarah's home with a babysitter for the day.

The party continued until about 5 p.m., when Bradley and Austin decided to leave. As they were pulling out of Ashley's driveway, James called Hannah to make sure they were still on for the next night, and he informed her that he could not wait to see her in her cap and gown. He knew what an achievement this had been for both of them and was excited to be finally graduating from college.

The next morning, Hannah went down to get the title of the new Mustang changed into her name. Knowing it might take a while, she left early and got there just as they opened. She waited in line for about 45 minutes before they called her number and got the title changed. After paying the fee, she left and went by her new house. She had left Mark David with Sarah while she ran some errands and had promised to pick up some lunch for herself, Brandon, and Sarah before coming back to the house.

While at her new house, she called the utility companies and switched everything into her name. She had let herself into the house and was sitting on the bare floor of the living room, when she decided to get satellite television for the home. She would wait to order that until she actually moved in and could not do that for a few more days when the furniture arrived. Sarah had scheduled the interior decorator to come on Tuesday and had told them what they had purchased while giving them free rein on the rest of the house. Hannah began putting the pot and pans into the lower cabinets and arranging the silverware drawer when she looked at the time. It was almost 12:30 p.m., and she had not gotten lunch yet. She quickly finished putting things away and left to go get lunch. She made it back to Sarah's and immediately started apologizing for her lateness. She had stopped to get hamburgers and fries from a local fast-food restaurant and the line had been long, but she got them lunch as promised.

Over lunch, Sarah suggested they take a nap before the graduation ceremony that night and Hannah liked the idea. Hannah informed Sarah about how much she had gotten done that morning and knew there was a lot more to do before she could move into her new house. Sarah told her Hannah had a good start and that she and Ashley would help her in any way they could. After lunch, Sarah asked Brandon to be a good big brother and lay Robert down for a nap and then lay down for a nap himself. Brandon was happy to do this. Hannah laid Mark David down, then went to her room and laid down also. She set her alarm so she could take a shower before meeting up with James and going to the graduation ceremony.

Shortly before her alarm went off, Sarah heard the doorbell ring and knew it would be Kinsey, the babysitter, coming for the night. Sarah cussed under her breath about oversleeping and went to answer the door. As she let Kinsey in, she explained that Ashley was going to bring the twins over and that Kinsey would have two toddlers to also watch that night. Sarah knew this would be extra work and told Kinsey that her appreciation would be shown at the end of the night. Kinsey had no problem with this, knowing that Sarah always paid good and that the children were usually well-behaved. She also knew Brandon was a good big brother and uncle and tried to take care of the babies himself. He was always a lot of help.

At 5 p.m., Ashley and the twins arrived followed shortly by Tim. Sarah introduced Ashley and the twins to Kinsey and saw that the girls took to her right away. Dave arrived home and told everyone that the reservations at Rusty's were for 6 p.m. They would go eat and get to the graduation ceremony by 7 p.m. Hannah knew she was supposed to meet James outside the auditorium at 7 p.m. and suggested she take her own car that night. She also explained that she might have to leave the restaurant a little early to get to the ceremony. They all understood and

Sarah remembered James was supposed to meet her there. Sarah began to crack a little smile at the thought.

Dinner was ordered as soon as they were seated. Hannah, being nervous, only ordered a grilled chicken salad with ranch dressing on the side. She did not know if her stomach would let her eat that night, but she had to try. After their dinners arrived, they conversed about how their days had gone and how excited they were that Hannah was graduating with her bachelor's degree. At one point, Sarah asked her if she was planning to return to school for her master's degree and Hannah said she was looking into some online schools that she could attend at night from the comfort of her new home.

After she ate most of her salad, Hannah excused herself and headed for the college auditorium. She had gotten to know James a little bit over the phone these last couple of nights and had found out that they have similar tastes in music and similar values in life. She had explained why she was living with Sarah. Hannah explained that Ashley, Sarah, and their husbands had gotten her a house. She also explained how they had unofficially adopted her and that she was now part of the family. She informed him that now she had two big brothers that would track him down if he did anything to hurt her, and one was a lawyer and the other had the land to hide a body. She explained how she had met Sarah by answering a want ad about a tutor and that she thought of Brandon as her little brother. Hannah even explained that since she moved in with Sarah, she had not been charging her for tutoring sessions, but that Sarah had been paying a lot of Hannah's bills and giving her the money to survive with. Hannah loved Sarah and truly felt that they were sisters in a past life and knew they were more than just good friends in this life. Hannah knew Sarah had saved her from a bad situation and knew she could never repay her for all she had done in such a short time. She felt the same for Ashley, too.

They talked for half an hour, then had to get to their seats and get ready for their graduation ceremony. After the caps had been tossed, James found her and asked if she wanted to go for a cup of coffee or a soda. He explained some of his friends and him were going to Pizza King to hang out for old times' sake and asked her to come along. She politely turned him down saying she had to get back to Mark David and pay the babysitter. He understood and said he would call her that night as they parted ways.

Hannah met up with Sarah, Ashley, Tim, and Dave in the parking lot and talked to them for a minute before heading back to Sarah's house. Hannah beat the rest of them home and went ahead and paid Kinsey what she thought she was worth: $200. This covered the time she was at the house and a little extra for watching Ashley's children. She knew it was a large sum and that Kinsey's going rate was only $10/hour, but she wanted to really show how much she appreciated all that Kinsey did for her and Sarah.

That night, James did call her, and they wound up talking until after midnight. The next morning, Hannah awoke to a phone call from Ryan, saying that he wanted to see his son that coming weekend. He said he had a change of heart and wanted to build a relationship with him. He knew there was no repairing the relationship between Hannah and him, but he could be the father to his own son. He knew it was his right according to the divorce decree, but he did not want to force the point, so he politely asked Hannah to allow him what the judge had ordered. She said she would have to think about it and would get back to him that night with an answer. She wanted to talk to Dave and Sarah about the situation first, but did not tell Ryan this. Sarah had been in the courtroom, as the divorce and the paternity results were read. She had seen the young man blow his stack and get jail time for his outburst in court. Sarah had actually feared for Hannah's safety afterwards. She suggested to Hannah that this weekend they do a supervised visitation and slowly work into the weekend custody. Dave agreed that was the best idea. He did not trust Ryan at all. Hannah called Ryan and explained the supervised visitation idea, and he understood. He had made an ass of himself in court both times and accepted Hannah's decision. They agreed to meet at Sarah's house on Sunday afternoon after her tutorial session at the shelter and give him a couple of hours with his son.

The rest of the week seemed to flash by for Hannah. Before she knew it, she was going to the shelter to tutor on Saturday morning. Bradley noticed that she was a little distracted when she arrived and asked if she was okay. She told him about meeting James and their upcoming date.

"Girls!" Bradley said with a groan.

"Hey, we went out, too, you remember," Austin spoke from behind her.

"And I was nervous then also," Hannah said frankly.

"Did you inform him about the three rules?" Austin and Bradley asked simultaneously.

She did not answer, but just turned and walked down the hall to the tutoring room. That day, Austin suggested they all go to Pizza King again for lunch and to talk. Hannah enjoyed their company but wasn't sure she wanted pizza twice in one day. She decided to go with her friends anyway. They talked about what had been going on the last week in each of their lives and Hannah told them about the graduation gifts she had gotten, including the house. She went on to explain that it might be a month or so before she can totally move into her new house with the construction and everything. She also told them about Ryan's phone call and what they had worked out. She further explained that she was nervous about it, but that he was the father and had a right to see his son. After lunch, they went back to the shelter and continued tutoring.

She was supposed to meet James that evening, and the closer it got the more nervous she got. They had spent countless hours talking on the phone and had seen each other at their graduation, but this was going to be an official date and that always made her nervous. She started thinking that she was going to do or say something stupid and that would be the end of that relationship. Austin caught up to her as they were clocking out that day and wished her the best of luck on her date. Then, he gave her a hug and a kiss on the cheek saying that he would not mind another date with her sometime. This made her blush, and as she tried to hide the fact that she was turning beet red, Bradley stepped up and told her the same thing. She didn't know what to think now. She had three guys that wanted to date her, and she liked all three of them. She tried to push it out of her mind and just concentrate on driving, when her phone rang. It was James asking her if she could be at Pizza King a little early. He was already there and waiting for her. He told her that he knew that it was an hour and a half early, but he could not wait to see her again. She decided not to go home and change for the date and just headed to the restaurant.

When she arrived, she noticed where James was sitting right away and then spotted the bouquet sitting on the table with him.

"You are looking good tonight," James said as he handed her the flowers.

"Thank you but I didn't get a chance to go home and change. This is what I wore to work this morning and. . .," she started saying.

"You must be popular at the shelter," James interrupted. "You look good enough to eat."

She giggled at his words and his attempt at flirting with her, then she sat down at the table.

They talked for a while before ordering their food and even more after it arrived. Their date seemed to be going well, until she got a phone call from a private number.

"Watch out. I am coming for you and your child," a distorted voice on the other end said then disconnected the line.

This unnerved her and she called Sarah to check on Mark David. She was frantic when Sarah answered on the third ring and explained to her about the phone call. Sarah told her that Mark David was okay, in her arms and playing right then. She also made a mental note to tell her about the other phone calls and letters they had gotten when she returned home that evening. Sarah knew that Hannah was on a date at the time and did not want to upset her any more than she already was. She told her to go back to her date, and they would talk that night. Everything was fine.

Hannah really could not shake off the feeling of being watched nor the feeling that something was wrong with her child, so she decided to cut the date short. She explained the phone call and her feelings to James as best she could, hoping that he would understand. He did. He told her to go home, see her son, and that he would call her that night. They hugged and she left for

Sarah's house. When she arrived at Sarah's, the first thing she did was hug Mark David and give him a big kiss telling him that mommy loved him. Sarah had a small pile of letters on the couch next to her along with a small notebook. She started explaining them, even though she had no clue who it was doing this nor why; she laid out everything for Hannah to see. She even showed her the picture with the sticky note still on it. She knew she had been watched, but not sure when or why. There were more questions than answers about this whole ordeal and now this sicko was starting to harass Hannah. This made Sarah mad. She did not understand what Hannah, Tim or even herself had to do with why this person was doing this. She knew it had something to do with Dave and probably involved a pissed off person who did not get their way in a family matter be it a divorce, child custody, or even an adoption, but why bring the others into this and how did the person keep getting their private numbers. The questions came with very little answers. They had notified the police about the incidents and were told that no threat had been made, so there was really nothing they could do at the time. Now a threat had been made and it was against an innocent person and her young child.

Sarah notified the police about the latest incident and got an officer en route to the house. During this time, Dave had been out with Tim and Ashley having dinner, so she called them and asked them to come over explaining that the police were on their way. They left the restaurant they were at and headed towards Sarah's house. They arrived about three minutes before the police officer. As Dave and the others entered the house, they saw Hannah holding Mark David tightly in her arms crying and Sarah trying to console her. Ashley immediately sat on the other side of Hannah and wrapped her in her arms like Sarah had been doing.

They explained everything to the police officer and again they were told that patrol would be stepped up in the neighborhood and that there was no need to worry. This was just someone's sick joke and that the incidents may not even be connected to each other. The police officer made a report reluctantly and left the home. That night Hannah had Mark David sleep in bed with her.

When James called, she talked to him in a hushed tone as to not wake her sleeping child. She explained all that she had found out about the letters and other calls in a nervous tone of voice, then the conversation turned a little more light-hearted as he asked her for a second chance for a first date. He said that he hoped this time it would go better. She actually laughed after he made that statement, remembering the first date with Austin and how he had asked for a redo after kissing her. This put her in a better mood and lightened her spirits enough to talk to James for another hour or so. She had decided not to tell anyone else about the goings-on before she drifted off to sleep. That night, she dreamt of her son and James playing around together and enjoyed the dream.

She awoke the next morning refreshed and ready to take on the world, but knew she needed to shower and dress first. After her shower, she ate breakfast consisting of two hard-boiled eggs and a piece of toast, kissed Mark David goodbye, and headed to the shelter. On her way there, she had to stop for gas and grabbed some sodas for the day ahead. As she was checking out, Ryan called to confirm that they were still on for that evening so he could build a relationship with his child. She informed him that they were still on and that he needed to be at Sarah's no later than 6 p.m. that night. She also told him he would only have a couple of hours with their child, and he said that would be acceptable.

The day seemed to drag on at the shelter. There were not many people that wanted or needed a tutor that day and the three of them mostly sat around talking until lunch. They decided to have lunch at Rusty's that day instead of at Pizza King since they had that the previous day. As they arrived, Hannah asked if James was working and asked to be seated at one of his tables, not thinking about the two guys with her. James was surprised to see her there with two handsome guys as he approached the table.

"Boy, do I have some stiff competition," he said as he took their drink orders.

"James, these are two of my tutoring buddies at the shelter," she said, introducing each of them individually.

Austin and Bradley felt a little weird and jealous sitting at the table where the server was dating the same girl they had and would love to date again, but neither would let on. They ordered meals and started talking about how slow it had been at the shelter as James walked away. James did not know that these were the two guys she had dated after her divorce, but could see in their eyes that they both liked her a little bit more than as just friends. Although he was a little jealous himself, he did not let it affect his work, nor would he tell her afterwards when they talked that night. After their noon meal, they went back to the shelter and sat around for the rest of their shift with no tutoring sessions. Hannah had let the other tutors go home early, leaving just her, Austin, and Bradley to tutor if need be.

That night after the tutoring sessions, she drove home and hugged Mark David again, remembering the phone call she had gotten the night before. Sarah had made dinner for everyone, and they ate after Hannah finished bear hugging her son. Sarah had made pork chops in cream of mushroom gravy in the crock pot and some steamed rice to go along with it. She had also made a salad and a chocolate cake for dessert. She knew it was a simple meal, but she also knew they enjoyed this particular meal often. After they ate, Hannah helped clean up the kitchen as Sarah loaded the dishwasher, and Dave talked with Mark David about a visitor coming. The kitchen was finished and Mark David was starting to get antsy about the visitor.

Ryan arrived at the house hoping he had not interrupted their dinner. Dave let him in and told him that if he lost his temper in the slightest way then Ryan would be leaving and that Dave would be filing for full custody of Mark David on Hannah's behalf the next morning. Ryan said he understood and that he had changed over the last year or so. Mark David was a little shy at first around Ryan, but quickly warmed up to him as they sat on the couch together and Ryan read him a book that he had brought. After the story, Ryan actually got on the floor and played cars with his son and seemed to be enjoying himself. They played for the full two hours and then Dave said it was time for Mark David to go to bed. Ryan asked if he could help put him to bed and tuck him in for the night. After some consideration, Hannah said that would be okay. After they had tucked their child in for the night, Ryan asked if he could come over the next weekend to see him again. Hannah had some reservations, but agreed to let him come over on Sunday night again for a couple of hours. He thanked her as he left.

That night, when James called her, she told him about Ryan coming over and how Mark David had taken to him. She also told him that Ryan was going to see their son again the following weekend. Then they made plans for a second first date. James said he had Tuesday and Thursday off from work that week and asked which day would be better for Hannah.

"Why can't we go out both nights?" she asked in a flirtatious tone.

"Does that mean the competition I saw at lunch is no more?" he asked jokingly.

"No, it means that I can see them on other nights. There are more than two nights in a week you know," she retorted.

"Are you seeing other people on other nights?" he asked shyly.

"Nobody has asked me out lately, but a girl has to keep her options open until she finds the right guy. I am not ready to settle down just yet with just any Tom, Dick, or Harry. I need to see who could make me a good husband and Mark David a good dad," she said being completely honest with him.

"I understand how you feel. After all, the first guy or girl you date may not be the right one, but then again it might be. You can't rule that possibility out either, though," James said with a feeling of sorrow to his voice.

By the end of the call, she had agreed to see James on his days off, but not to tell him about any other guys she might be seeing. He had also agreed that he would keep his options open as well.

That next day, the furniture arrived at Hannah's house. Knowing that construction was going to take place on the main floor, she decided to have the bed placed in the office space of the basement. She could use the kitchenette in the basement to make her meals and refrigerate her groceries. Everything had been brought in and set up in 45 minutes and since she was a little tired, she decided to lay down to rest until the satellite company came at noon. She made the bed and laid down for about an hour. At noon, she was awakened by the ringing of her doorbell. The satellite company was right on time. After the installer had gotten some information from her about where she wanted the dish to be placed, he quickly set everything up and had her watching television within 30 minutes. She thought to herself that she was going to enjoy the house once everything was completed, and called Sarah to come over and see the progress that had been made. She started thinking about renting the basement out since it had its own outside entrance. She discussed the option with Sarah when she arrived, and they decided it would be a good idea.

"Are you going to bring anyone to the Fourth of July party at Ashley's house?" Sarah asked Hannah with a wry smile.

"I haven't decided yet. I might ask James, but then again, I might ask Austin to come," she replied obviously confused.

"Austin? Are you seeing him again?" Sarah asked bewildered.

"No, but he is a friend and I do like him. I have been thinking about seeing if he wants to go out sometime. I know we agreed to be friends, but I still see the way his eyes light up when he looks at me. I think he likes me more than just friends. As a matter of fact, so does Bradley. I could easily fall in love with any of the three. I have already explained the three simple rule to each of them, and they have all agreed to them. I don't know what to do. I definitely need some help with this situation," Hannah confessed.

"Three possible suitors. Damn girl, you are in a pickle," Sarah replied.

At two o'clock, the kitchen appliances showed up along with the kitchen hutch. Knowing that the kitchen would soon have demo and construction, they had them all placed in the garage. They sat in the living room and drank a couple of sodas as they talked the rest of the afternoon away. At a quarter to five, Sarah said she had to go pick up the children from daycare and Hannah decided to go along with her. She had to get Mark David from there also and then, when Dave got home, they would all go out to eat. Hannah had decided that when the house was completely finished, she would throw a party for all of her friends, including the three potential boyfriends, and hoped it did not break any of the three rules.

That night, Ashley, Tim, and the twins showed up at Sarah's house. Hannah informed Ashley about the progress at her house and the idea of renting the basement out as a one-bedroom apartment. Ashley suggested if she wanted to do that, then Hannah needed to get the basement its own electrical meter. That way, she could accurately charge for utilities. Hannah thought that would be a good idea, and said she would get on that the next morning while Sarah and her waited on the interior decorator to come in and look everything over. She knew this meant probably having to rewire the basement, or at least getting it on a separate breaker, but she was okay with that.

The general contractor arrived that morning and the interior decorator arrived just five minutes later. Sarah explained what they wanted done in the kitchen and basement and the general contractor informed them that it would take four weeks to complete the job. Sarah then talked to the interior decorator and informed them of the change in plans and asked if they could set the basement up as a separate apartment as well. They agreed and said they would tackle that after the contractor finished their work in the basement. Everything was going smoothly and the contractor actually started on the basement that day. He informed them that this way the interior decorator could start in the upstairs and work their way down, and he could work his way up. Neither of them would get into each other's way.

The interior decorator informed Sarah of the cost and said it would only take two days to a week, if they needed to paint, to fill the large house. The contractor said it would take about the same two days to set the apartment up for use. He then called the electrician and started getting the permits for the job. He said that he knew someone at city hall that could help hurry through the permits and could get the dual residency allowed that day. He advised Hannah that she would have to add a mailbox and set up the apartment with its own address, to which she asked if she could just use her address and put the letter A behind it. He said that would work. The contractor called the electrician and informed him to start that day on the basement area. He then turned his attention to the demolition in the kitchen.

Hannah and Sarah were able to get another mailbox that day before lunch.

"Where is the person in the apartment going to park?" Hannah asked over lunch.

"They can park in your driveway and walk to their door," Sarah responded.

"But the sidewalk doesn't go all the way to the basement door, and I was wondering about putting a driveway in on that side of the house with its own sidewalk," Hannah said dreamily.

"That's not a bad idea Hannah, not bad at all. After lunch, let's see if we can get that done in the next few days," Sarah spoke in a joyful tone.

That night, Hannah and James had their do-over first date. This time, he took her to Rusty's for dinner. They talked while they ate and decided to go to a movie afterward. At the end of the movie, James hugged her on their way out of the theater. She said she would see him on Thursday as they said their goodbyes. Hannah did not get back to Sarah's house until almost eleven that night. By that time, Mark David had already gone to bed, so she softly walked into his room and softly kissed him goodnight. James did not call that night due to it being so late. He did call her at 7:30 a.m. the next morning though.

"I had a lot of fun with you last night and I really do like you more each day," James confessed.

"I also had fun and I like you also," Hannah stated sleepily.

"Do you think we have a chance, I mean, in the long run?" he asked.

"I don't know, I can't tell the future, and officially, we have only been on one date so far. Don't you think you might be rushing it a little bit?" she spoke in a snarky tone.

"Obviously, you are not a morning person," he said with a bit of humor in his voice.

"Sorry about the tone, I am just now really waking up," she said through a yawn.

They talked for about 30 minutes and then had to get Mark David to the daycare for the day. She wanted to move in to her house as soon as the basement was completed and was anxious to get the day started.

That morning, Bradley called her and asked her out for lunch that day. He explained to her that it could just be a couple of friends going to lunch or, if she would like to, she could consider it a date. She liked the idea of it being another date with him and told him so. James worked the evening shift that day, so she agreed when Bradley suggested they meet at Rusty's for lunch. She arrived at Rusty's at five minutes to noon and saw Bradley already seated in the restaurant. She made her way over to him trying to remain calm.

She really did like Bradley and was nervous about going on a date with him. After all, they have been through dates before, and she needed time to get her life together. She hoped it was together enough to start dating Bradley again. She caught herself thinking about Austin over lunch and wondering if he would want to go out sometime again. Bradley could see the faraway look in her eyes and asked if everything was okay with her.

"Sorry, I was thinking about something else and not really giving you the date or time you deserve. I will push everything else aside and focus only on a handsome man who has asked me out," Hannah tried to explain without too many details.

She instead lied and explained that her new house was being worked on and there was a lot of stuff she had to get done rather quickly in order to move in. Bradley asked when she would be moved in fully, and she replied hopefully in a month. She then gave him a heads up about the party she would be having at her house. She asked him if he could come and to remind him that it was as friends only and that if he wanted to bring a date, he was more than welcome to do so. She informed him when the construction was done, she would let everyone know when the party would be. She then thought about asking him to come over to Ashley's for the Fourth of July party coming up in a couple of weeks. She knew that they all could take the weekend off at the shelter and thought about asking Austin to come as well. She needed to inform James soon so he could schedule the weekend off also, if she was going to invite them all as friends. She knew she could get another tent or two for the guys and that Ashley had always told her the more the merrier when it came to guests, but she still wanted to ask her first before any of the guys were asked. After they finished lunch, they said their goodbyes and went their separate ways.

Hannah headed to the shelter to talk to Ashley for permission to invite all the guys. She found Ashley sitting in a rocking chair, rocking a baby to sleep for a nap. Hannah quietly asked her about the party and Ashley asked her if she was still following the three simple rules. Hannah said she had been and would continue to follow them. Ashley asked if they would all sleep in the same tent and Hannah explained that she would purchase another tent for the guys to sleep in. She and Mark David would sleep in one tent alone and the boys in another. She promised promiscuity would not be happening that weekend and Ashley agreed to let her invite them all.

On her way out of the shelter, she started calling the guys. First, she called James and invited him as a friend and explained other guys would likely be there as well. He said that it sounded like a good time and that he would try to get the weekend off. Then she called Bradley and invited him. He was shocked that she had called him so soon after their date and said he would love to go as a friend. She saved the hardest for last, and once she built up enough courage, she called Austin. He did not answer right away but called her back within five minutes of her hanging up without leaving a voicemail. He was delighted to hear her voice and told her so. He apologized for not answering the phone a moment ago, but explained he had been busy with something and could not answer the phone at that particular moment. She explained to him the situation and invited him to come along. He said he would on one condition, and that was that she go out with him on a date again soon. She said yes to his condition and asked if Friday night would be soon enough. They made plans to meet at Rusty's on Friday night, and she started feeling a little giddy at the thought of dating Austin again.

The rest of the day she spent at Sarah's house and had agreed to stay there until the basement was completed, hopefully the next day. Sarah was excited about the men asking for dates and even more excited that they might all come to the Fourth of July party at Ashley's. She reminded Hannah to tell them to bring fishing poles and tackle boxes because they would probably do some fishing during the day Saturday and Sunday. Hannah knew that two of the three liked to fish, but was not sure about James. She would have to ask him on their date the next night, or over the phone if he called her that night. Austin called her about 7 p.m. that night and apologized for being a little forward earlier in the day. He had hoped she would forgive him for placing a condition on the Fourth of July party. He did not want her to think he was being mean or anything. He explained that he had been wanting to ask her out again for some time and it just seemed like a good idea at the time. She explained to him that they could date, but that they were not exclusive and that she would be dating other people for a while, at least until she was able to weed out some or find the one she wanted to settle down with. He reluctantly accepted her terms and said he would also be dating others. She could tell by the tone in his voice that was a lie and knew he wanted to become more of an item with her. Austin was a nice guy, and she liked him a little more than the others, but she was not ready to get serious with anyone at this point in her life. She knew things could always change, but for right now, that is the way she wanted it. She knew all three of the guys were looking forward to dating her and hoped not to hurt any of them when the time came.

Austin and Hannah talked on the phone for about an hour before she got another call. She looked and saw it was Bradley. She told Austin that she had to go for now and switched over to the other line to talk to Bradley. They talked about their date that day, and he admitted that he was happy that she had accepted his offer on such short notice. He told her that he liked her, and she explained that she was not settling on one boyfriend right now in her life. She explained to him there were others she would be dating and would eventually pick the one that she thought could be a possible good husband and a good father to Mark David, but that would be down the road somewhere. She also explained that she did not know how long that would take. She had to ask him to hold on for a minute, while she put Mark David to bed near the beginning of their phone call, then they talked for about an hour and a half.

Around 10 p.m. that night, James called and asked how her day had been. She would not go into a lot of details about much, but told him how the house was coming along. She informed him that she was getting excited to move in and have a party. She also informed him that Mark David was going to love his backyard and room. She also said that she was thinking about putting a playground in for him and James said that would be a good idea. They talked for a little while, then Hannah got another call. This time it was Ryan. She asked James to hold the line while she talked to him for a minute and switched over to Ryan.

Ryan said he was calling to inform her that he had been going to anger management classes and also a counselor because of the way he had demanded sex from her. He wanted her to know that he had indeed changed and asked if he could prove it by taking her and Mark David out Sunday night instead of just having visitation. He even went as far as to ask her if she was seeing anyone special at the time. She told him that she was dating around with several guys and that she would allow him to take her and Mark David out Sunday night. She also informed him that they were not dating, but just going to be parents to their young son.

After she got off the phone, she switched back to James and talked to him for about another 20 minutes before getting off to go to sleep. She needed to talk to Sarah and Ashley about Ryan and the other guys, but did not know how to broach the subject of Ryan safely. She decided to talk with Sarah first thing the next morning, and then she could go to the shelter and talk to Ashley.

Thursday morning, she had changed her mind about talking to Sarah. She would talk to Ashley first thing that day. She knew she would be seeing Sarah at her house later that morning and decided that would be a better time and place to talk with her. Hannah dressed quickly and got Mark David ready for daycare. Then she informed Sarah that she had some errands to run and would meet her at the house later in the morning. She packed up her beautiful child and left for the daycare.

Once at the shelter, she found Ashley changing a baby's diaper and started to explain the sticky situation she was in. She first told Ashley about the three guys and all that they said the previous night over the phone. She explained that she liked all three of them, but did not know what to do about dating them. She told Ashley that she wanted to narrow down her prospect list, but did not want to hurt any of them. After she talked for almost 20 minutes about the three guys, she decided to tell Ashley the real reason she has come to see her.

"Now, there is an even bigger problem than all that. Ryan called me last night as well. He wanted to take me and Mark David out Sunday night," Hannah started explaining.

"What did you say?" Ashley asked.

"Well, I kind of agreed to it. I know what he did in the past, but I think that I still love him. We were together for over two years, and he is the father of my child. I honestly believe that he has changed back to the guy I fell in love with long ago. I am not saying that I am willing to let everything that has happened just go out the window, but. . .," Hannah said with her head hung low in shame.

"You want to give him a chance to prove to you that he has changed. don't you?" Ashley stated with compassion and understanding.

"Well, yes. I kind of do. Like I said, I still love him and probably always will. What do I do? I haven't told Sarah yet because I am pretty sure she will kill me for the way that I am feeling. I came to you first because I trust you and I know you are more impartial that Sarah. You are more understanding when it comes to the matters of the heart, I think, and you can help me figure out how to tell her. I do want her opinion just as much as I wanted yours, but I don't want her to kill me afterwards." Hannah said as she realized that she was starting to ramble.

As Hannah finally took a breath, she noticed the smile on Ashley's face. Then it was Ashley's turn to talk.

"I do understand. I dated a guy in high school that I thought that I loved. I dated him for almost two years, my junior and senior years as a matter of fact. We did everything together. One day, he finally convinced me to have sex with him. After that, he dropped me like a dirty diaper. What I found out later is that he had made a bet with one of his friends that he was going to have sex with me and take my virginity before the end of high school or else he would pay the friend a hundred dollars. I was just a prize to be had for him and that is why I started the three simple rules. Now, in your case, things are different. You followed the three simple rules and still got a raw deal out of it. You have two choices as I see it. One, give in to your feelings and give Ryan another chance, but if you do that you need to start the rules all over again. Then, there is the second option. You could date around and see what comes out of the wash. The choice is yours, but if it were me, I would go with the first option and give him a chance. People do change and I believe Ryan can be a good husband and a good father. Maybe he just had some issues he needed to work out. You are both young and just starting out your lives." Ashley said as she held Hannah close to her.

Hannah agreed to take Ashley's advice into consideration and left the shelter to return to her house. She was already running a little late meeting up with Sarah. Once Hannah got to her house, she found Sarah in the front yard with the power company representative, who was adding a second meter to the side of the house.

"The basement is ready for you to move into, or you can start looking to rent it out to someone else and stay with me until the construction is complete," Sarah stated.

"Can we talk for a moment in private?" Hannah bashfully asked.

"Sure, let's go inside and talk about whatever put that sour face on you," Sarah said a little nervously.

Once inside, Hannah laid out the situation to Sarah, about all four guys and the fact that she liked all of them. She asked for her advice, after telling her what Ashley had said a little earlier that morning. Sarah tended to agree with Ashley and stated that the best way out of this sticky situation was to follow the three simple rules and be honest with everyone.

"What do you think about asking Ryan to Ashley's house for the weekend of the Fourth?" Hannah asked timidly.

"Do you trust him enough right now to have him around your other suitors? Do you think he will be okay around the other guys, or do you think it will become a pissing contest between the four of them?" she asked being blunt.

Sarah's questions gave Hannah a lot to think about. Getting the three guys she was already dating together was going to be difficult enough. Then to add her ex-husband into the mix, just might start another world war. It was decided that Hannah would see Ryan that Sunday night with their son present and that she would see where it goes from there. She felt a little bad about not inviting Ryan to the weekend-long party, but it did make sense not to have him there right now. They had been apart for about a year, and they needed to start over fresh. Hannah also decided to stay at Sarah's house for the next month or so until the construction was completed. She also stated that she might sleep a night or two at her house, but would mostly be at Sarah's.

Sarah's cell phone rang at 3:15 p.m. As she looked at the caller ID, she noticed that the caller was calling from Dexter's Methodist Hospital.

She answered, not sure of what to expect, maybe a question on their insurance or a billing inquiry.

"Hello?" she said as she answered the call.

"Hello, is this Mrs. Sarah Palmer?" the voice on the other end asked.

"Yes, this is Sarah Palmer," she stated.

"This is Doctor Rathsmason at Methodist Hospital Emergency Department; I am sorry to inform you that your husband has been shot and is in critical condition. You may want to come down and see him. . .," the caller said.

"Dave. . . is he okay, how bad is it?" she said in a hurried tone as tears started flowing down her face.

"Ma'am, he has lost a lot of blood and we have him stabilized at the moment, but he is in critical condition, like I said. He is going for emergency surgery in a few minutes, but we don't know anything else at this time. You can see him when he comes out of surgery and is in a recovery room. Surgery should take about an hour and then another half an hour for him to wake up from anesthesia. He will be located in room ICU 2458. We can give you more information when you get here," Dr Rathsmason said.

Sarah hung up the phone and started bawling right in front of Hannah. Hannah held her tight and tried to comfort and calm her friend. Once

Sarah had calmed enough to explain the phone call to Hannah, she did. Hannah immediately called Ashley, informing her about the call. Hannah asked that Ashley get a hold of Tim and have them meet her and Sarah at the hospital as soon as possible. She called Kinsey over to babysit the children. She then told Sarah she would drive her to the hospital, and they were on their way.

Once they got to the hospital, Ashley was already in the surgery recovery waiting room waiting on Hannah and Sarah to arrive. She informed them that Tim had been in a meeting, but he should be there in a few minutes. Sarah asked the nurse at the reception desk for more information on the status of her husband, and was told the surgeon would come out and talk to her as soon as he was out of surgery. Sarah was a nervous wreck and sat crying throughout the long wait. She had Hannah go down to the cafeteria to get everyone something to drink and asked her to get her a couple of cups of coffee with cream.

"I need to calm down and the hospital won't allow me to drink wine, so coffee will have to do," Sarah said in an attempt at humor in the situation.

Ashley took Hannah's place holding and comforting her friend while she went for the drinks. Hannah and Ashley were trying to hold it together also, but Hannah knew Ashley would be needing to be strong for her dear friend. Hannah got Ashley's order from her and asked what Tim might want when he got there. She hurried to the cafeteria, got the drinks, and headed back to the recovery area. When she got back, Tim was walking in the doors. She saw him and led him to where the ladies were sitting. She dispensed the drinks to everyone and sat an extra cup of coffee on the chair next to Sarah. About an hour later, the surgeon came out and talked to Sarah.

"Mrs. Palmer, your husband is doing good and is awake if you want to see him. He came through surgery fine and will be in the ICU for at least the night. He was shot in the chest and the bullet missed his heart and major arteries by mere millimeters, but he is still in critical condition. Have the police officers talked to you yet?"

"No, nobody has talked to us yet. You are the first," she responded with anxiety in her voice.

"Only family can come back and see him right now, so we don't overwhelm him," the surgeon stated.

"We are all his family," Sarah stated in a matter-of-fact tone.

"Okay, just please don't upset him and be aware, that he may drift in and out of consciousness as a result of the anesthetics and the surgery he just went through," the surgeon said, as he led them to the recovery room.

Once in the recovery room, Sarah gently held Dave's hand, and she looked at all the wires attach to him. He was hooked up to a heart monitor and had three bottles of fluid running through the IV. One being blood and another was saline solution. She figured the last must be pain medication. He could not talk but was alert enough to squeeze her hand when she said his name. They stayed in the room for about a half an hour before transport came to take him to his room in ICU. Once in the ICU room, only one visitor was allowed at a time, so Sarah went in first. She sat with him for over an hour before he started talking to her.

"He just came in my office and told me I was dead. He then shot me. What the hell happened after that I don't know," Dave said in a raspy voice struggling to talk.

As soon as he said that, the nurse came in and informed Sarah that there were two police officers, wanting to talk to her outside in the waiting room.

"I will be right back honey; I have to go talk to the cops for a minute," she said giving him a light kiss on his cheek as she left the room.

"Mrs. Palmer, I am Officer Jack Morgan. Your husband's attacker has been caught and is in custody downtown, as we speak. Apparently, his wife used your husband's services for a divorce some time ago, and he has plotted revenge for some time now. He has already confessed to shooting your husband and also confessed to sending him letters in the mail as well as harassing you and your family. He has been stalking Mr. Palmer for months and finally worked up the nerve to do this heinous act today. We caught him still in your husband's office just sitting on the floor where your husband had fallen. The secretary called 911 when she heard the shot and the ambulance got there just in the nick of time. He remained alert until he was placed in the ambulance, and we got the suspect into custody," Officer Morgan stated.

After the officers left, Hannah told Sarah that she would go pick up the children and take them home for the night, giving Sarah the night to spend with Dave. Sarah asked about her date with James, and she stated that she had already called him and canceled due to the circumstances. He understood. He told her to take care of Sarah and that he would call her later that night once the children were in bed. Sarah informed everyone that the nurse had told her that Dave might be in the hospital for about a week and that tonight was just a precautionary measure. Dave would most likely be moved to a regular room the next morning. Ashley and Tim stayed for about another hour and then left for the shelter to pick up their twins, then went home themselves.

They all got little sleep that night because they were worrying about how Sarah was handling things. James called Hannah about 9 p.m. that night, and they talked about Dave and Sarah for about an hour and a half. Hannah got emotional, while talking to him several times and started crying. James did his best to calm her down and soothe her, but in the end, it was all in vain. She had held it in all afternoon and evening, now she finally had a chance to let the pain and frustration out. So, she did. After the phone call, she called Sarah and checked in on how Dave was doing. Sarah informed her that he was sleeping and that everything was looking good according to the nurses. They talked for a few minutes then Sarah said she was going to try to get some sleep, and they hung up telling each other goodnight.

The next day, Dave was moved to a regular room in the hospital after the doctors checked in on him that morning. Sarah called everyone and informed them of his new location. They were all glad that he was doing better. Hannah asked if she could come down and relieve Sarah for a little while, so Sarah could go home and get a little rest and clean up. Sarah loved the thought and said she would be waiting for Hannah to show up. Hannah gathered all the children and took them to the daycare, then went directly to the hospital to meet Sarah. Dave had a nice private room with a view. He was more talkative this morning and told Sarah that he loved her as she left. He then thanked Hannah for all that she had done and was still doing for them both. Hannah stayed with him for about five hours, and they talked between Dave's naps. Sarah arrived back at the hospital refreshed and with a pillow and blanket so she could sleep on the pull-out couch that night. Sarah and Hannah talked for a while and then Hannah needed to go pick up the children and get them fed for the night. On her way out, she informed Sarah that she was canceling all her dates until Dave was feeling better and at home. That way, she could take care of the children at night and let Sarah have a break daily while Dave was in the hospital.

It continued that way for the next four days. That's when Dave got released from the hospital and was finally able to go home. His discharge papers said he needed to rest and not exert himself for another week or so and not to lift anything over 10 pounds. They gave him a prescription for pain medicine and told him if he did not need it, don't take it.

Hannah called Ryan once Dave was settled in at home and apologized to him again for not being able to meet up the previous Sunday night. She promised to make it up to him, and he asked her if she could make it Wednesday night. She agreed, and they talked for a while about how Dave was doing and if they needed anything or any help. He truly seemed to care and this tugged at Hannah's heart strings. After the phone call, she informed Sarah about the call and asked for Kinsey's phone number, explaining that she wanted to have Kinsey watch the children at Hannah's house the next night while she was out with Ryan. She wanted to give Sarah and Dave a night alone after such an ordeal. Sarah thanked her and gave her Kinsey's number. Kinsey was saddened to hear about Dave being shot, but was available for Wednesday night and Hannah gave Kinsey her new address. Hannah also explained about the construction in the kitchen but explained that the basement was fully stocked and the television worked on the main floor. She further explained that the only bed was in the basement and that it was big enough for all the children to sleep on. Kinsey agreed to be there at 5 p.m. and watch the children.

That night, Dave had a hard time sleeping due to the pain and the fact that he was not taking the pain medicine. So, he sat up in his office at home, reading over past and current client's files. He was determined not to let another mistake happen that could end up like this. He did not ever want to put Sarah through anything like this again. This was the second time he nearly lost his life, and he did not want there to be a third time.

Around 3 a.m. that morning he heard someone walking down the stairs and figured that it was Sarah looking for him. He met her at his home office door and explained he could not sleep. They sat up for a while together talking. Then about the time the sun started coming up, they both went back to bed. Sarah first went to Hannah's room and asked her to be a sweetheart and watch the children that morning, explaining that they had not slept well. Hannah said it was no problem and the least that she could do as she got up and started getting dressed for the day.

That night, Hannah packed the children up and took them over to her house at four thirty. Kinsey arrived at five minutes to five and Hannah showed her around the house. Hannah's date was set for six o'clock, and she had decided not to take Mark David with her this time. She wanted to see if Ryan had actually changed or not. She also wanted to be able to talk to him while being candid about everything. She knew that a child would only cause barriers in the conversation, and she did not want that tonight. She needed to find out, once and for all, what his intentions were.

She left the children with Kinsey and headed to the restaurant to meet up with Ryan. She arrived 15 minutes early and got a table in the back so they could talk in a little bit of privacy. Ryan arrived shortly thereafter and was surprised that Mark David was not there. She explained that he would have another chance to see their child that weekend, but this was her time tonight to clear the air on many things. He said he understood and welcomed the evening alone with her, so he could get some things off his chest as well.

As they placed their order they began to talk:

"If you don't mind, I would like to start and explain a few things. I first want to thank you for divorcing me when you did. What I did to you was inexcusable. I demanded something that I should not have and treated you like a possession and not like my wife, nor like a human being. What you don't know is that just before we were married, I started using drugs, cocaine to be exact, and it made me feel superior to everyone. I thought that I deserved everything and that I just had to take it for it to be mine. I thought women were just good for one thing and that was only with their legs spread. I am ashamed of what I did and how I felt and have no excuse for my actions, but I did get help. When I went to jail for the 30 days, after the paternity results came in, was the first time I had been sober that entire year. I had a problem and just did not know how to face it, nor did I realize the toll I would be paying for my actions. After I got out of jail, I went into a drug treatment center and got cleaned up. So, I do thank the judge in our case for starting me on the right path back to who I truly am. I have worked hard and come along way, but now I am trying to make amends with you and our child. I still love you and would like nothing more than to get back together with you, but I don't know if you will allow that or not. I love our son and truly want to be a father to him and in his daily life. I don't know if you can forgive me or not for what I have done, but I just ask for the chance to prove to you I am back to the same guy you fell in love with before. My father did not kick me out of the house because I got married. He kicked me out because he found my stash of coke and got mad.

He is giving me a second chance and that is all I am asking of you," Ryan said getting choked up.

"I knew something had changed in you, kind of like a light switch being turned on. I did not know about the drug use, but it did hurt when you left me for someone else and shacked up with her right away. I am guessing she gave you what you wanted that I had refused you. I thought that our entire relationship was just a ploy to get into my pants and all you wanted from me was sex. I was furious with you and almost tried to leave you off the birth certificate, but Dave talked me out of it saying that everyone should have a father even if he walked out on me. Mark David has been a blessing to me and I do want you in his life, but I am not sure you deserve to be in his life. I came here tonight alone to find out several things and now I know some answers. I am going to give you the chance to prove to me that you have changed, but I warn you, you mess up and start acting like you did again, I will drop you like a hot potato. Do you understand? I will also let you know I am seeing other guys and if you want to win me back, it is not going to be easy. We can start over, but that includes the three simple rules will start over as well. This does not count as a first date either. This is just a clearing the air meeting and if you want to take on the role of one of my suitors, then you will have to make the right moves. I do still care about you, but I am going to be extra cautious about you as well." Hannah stated matter-of-factly.

"In all honesty, the girl I left you for was my dealer, and she offered me drugs for sex. I thought I had a win-win and wound-up screwing everything up. The only thing I did right in that situation was to get out eventually. I know I messed up, and for that, I am truly sorry. I will make it up to you and I would like to try to win you back. I know it is not going to be easy, but I also know you are worth the effort," Ryan said as he softly held her hand.

They talked more during dinner and Ryan asked for a chance at a first date with her for the following weekend. She agreed on this coming Friday night, and they agreed to meet at Rusty's at 6 p.m. for dinner. She also told him that it would take some time before she would bring Mark David on their dates, but that he could see their child still under supervised visitation for now. She did not want to take that away from Ryan, and she knew he could become a good dad.

Around eight o'clock, they finally left the restaurant and headed their separate ways. Once Hannah got back to her house, she paid Kinsey for her time and gathered the children and their belongings and headed the three blocks to Sarah's house. Sarah and Dave were sitting in the living room when Hannah pulled in the drive. As Hannah walked in with the children, Sarah saw that Brandon was carrying Robert and having a tough time doing so. She got up to help, but Brandon said he was the big brother and could do it. He made it to the stairs and that is when Sarah took over. Both Sarah and Hannah put their children to bed for the night, then returned to the living room to discuss the evening events.

Hannah started by telling Dave, what had been going on between her and Ryan. He was not overly thrilled about the situation, but could not interfere with Hannah's personal life. He sat and listened as she began talking. Sarah had already told Dave about the meeting that night, but did not know about the details discussed over dinner. She left that up to Hannah to inform them both. Hannah relayed what Ryan had told her and the options she had given him. Dave interrupted her only once, to ask if she still had feelings for him, to which she answered honestly and said she did. She then informed them that she had accepted a date with him for Friday night and that would count as the first date in their new relationship. She further explained that she had informed

Ryan that the three simple rules started over again and would be strictly adhered to.

Both Dave and Sarah had questions about everything and started asking them. Dave was excited to hear that Ryan had been a complete gentleman and did not even try to kiss her. Dave knew the three simple rules had started over and feared that Ryan would try to jump ahead of the game and try something. To his delight, Ryan had obeyed the ground rules. Sarah could see the look in Hannah's eyes when she would talk about Ryan and reminded her not to get too attached too quickly. There were still other men to date, and the more she dated, the better the fish she would catch. Sarah suggested that she only date one guy a week and have them take turns trying to impress her. She did not want Hannah to get hurt again by any of them. It took about two hours for Hannah to answer them all and by that time, they were ready to get a good night's sleep. They retired to their perspective rooms and told each other good night.

Life returned to normal more over the next two weeks, as Dave healed up enough to start thinking about returning to work. He decided to try limited hours after the Fourth of July weekend shindig at Ashley's place. He knew he was feeling better, but still not back to 100 percent, and he knew that he needed to be there for his family and friends. Besides all of that, he was looking forward to the Fourth of July camping trip at Ashley's.

The weekend of the Fourth of July, Hannah, Sarah, Dave, and the children left for Ashley's house at 5 p.m. that afternoon. They stopped by the store on their way for a few supplies, mostly hot dogs and beer. They arrived at Ashley's knowing that the guys would arrive the next day around lunchtime. Sarah and Hannah walked to the pond to set up tents once they arrived, leaving Dave at the house with Tim and Ashley. Sarah had gotten a blow-up mattress for everyone, especially for Dave, because he needs the extra support more right now. As they finished setting everything up, Dave walked out of the woods with Ashley, Tim, and the children in tow. Dave tried to help Tim gather firewood, but was told to sit by Tim. After the fire got started, they ate a couple of hot dogs and talked until bed time.

The next day, the other guests started arriving and followed the signs that Tim and Ashley had posted, showing the way to the pond. Bradley was the first to arrive. He brought his own tent and cooler along with an overnight bag and bedding for the camping trip. He said his fishing pole was still in his car back at the house and that after he finished setting everything up, he would go get it. When he returned from the house, he was walking alongside of Austin and James, each with their own tents and supplies. Bradley was carrying three fishing poles and three tackle boxes. The two latecomers set up their tents and bedding, then Hannah asked if anyone wanted to go swimming. Dave elected not to go in the water because of the recent surgery and said he would stay back and watch the children. Ashley stated that she too would stay back and help Dave. The others quickly changed into their bathing suits in the tents and got into the water on that hot Saturday. They swam for a couple of hours and then sat on the beach drying off talking to each other. James confessed that he thought it might be a little weird camping and hanging out with the other guys that Hannah was dating, and Austin explained that on that particular weekend, they all were just friends. Hannah spoke up and said that she hoped they all were friends and that she hoped they would remain that way.

They all talked until Tim started a dinner of hamburgers and hot dogs. After they ate, Bradley asked Brandon if he wanted to go fishing for a little while. Brandon quickly grabbed his small fishing pole and said for Bradley to "hurry up the fish are calling." They walked down the beach a little way and sat on the beach fishing. Brandon caught the first and only fish that night and would not let his new friend forget it. Around dusk, they started setting up the fireworks and got ready for the show. The fireworks show lasted about an hour with the children oohing and aahing at every explosion. Even the littlest ones seemed to enjoy the show. After the show, they put the children to bed and sat around the fire talking and drinking coffee and beer. They talked about a lot of things, but Hannah's dating life never came up. They were all becoming good friends.

The next morning, they awoke to the smell of fish frying and Ashley sitting by the fire pit cooking them all breakfast. James asked her how long she had been up, and she replied about two hours. That was enough time to catch six fish. They all ate the fish for breakfast and played with the children that morning. Dave decided to try his hand at fishing after breakfast and caught a couple right away. He released them back into the pond and said that was enough excitement for his day.

As the day went on, they started to pack up and head their different ways with each of the guys thanking Ashley for the hospitality and telling Tim that they enjoyed their weekend.

Sarah, Dave, and the children left around 3 p.m. because Dave needed to rest up for work the next day. Hannah was the last to leave, and before she left, she asked Ashley if she needed any help with anything and received a "no" response.

Life resumed over the next two weeks until Hannah got a call from the contractor saying the house was finished. She could start moving in on Friday of that week. Hannah felt this was bittersweet because she loved being with Sarah and everyone, but knew she needed to be on her own as well. She informed Sarah, and they started planning a housewarming party for the following weekend.

To be continued

Made in the USA
Columbia, SC
06 October 2022

68885713R00138